THE RELUCTANT DETECTIVE

THE
RELUCTANT
DETECTIVE

A FAITH MORGAN MYSTERY

Martha Ockley

With special thanks to Rebecca Jenkins

MONARCH
BOOKS

Oxford, UK & Grand Rapids, Michigan, USA

First published in the UK in 2010 by Monarch Books
(a publishing imprint of Lion Hudson plc)
Wilkinson House, Jordan Hill Road, Oxford OX2 8DR, England
Tel: +44 (0)1865 302750 Fax: +44 (0)1865 302757
Email: monarch@lionhudson.com
www.lionhudson.com

ISBN 978 1 85424 985 2

Distributed by:
UK: Marston Book Services, PO Box 269, Abingdon, Oxon, OX14 4YN
USA: Kregel Publications, PO Box 2607, Grand Rapids, Michigan 49501

British Library Cataloguing Data
A catalogue record for this book is available from the British Library.

Printed and bound in the UK by MPG Books Ltd.

For Kate Morgan and Lulu Purda,
two of my favourite Kiwis.

CHAPTER

1

"You know I don't like to complain." Pat Montesque screwed up her soft cheeks into a fierce smile. "But I'll tell you, Elsie, I was a tad put out. I've always done the altar arrangements – since before Vicar Alistair came. You need a good substantial block of colour and there she was putting up a great waxy lily and a couple of twigs. Striking simplicity! I ask you!"

Elsie Lively tut-tutted sympathetically. She was looking at her dear Arthur's grave: probably thinking it needed a bit of a tidy, thought Pat. But then it was so difficult to get down on your knees at her age and well nigh impossible to get back up.

"Naturally I pointed out it wouldn't do – not in that space. Who's going to notice a single lily? The altar would be as good as bare. *He* said it was a misunderstanding. She'd only meant to help. Men!" She philosophized aloud. "What they don't know about women! And as for men of the cloth…"

"Charitable."

"What did you say, dear? Didn't quite catch that." Pat leaned down to the small, bent woman at her side with all the gracious condescension of a church officer to a valued lay member.

"Charitable – man of the cloth; a good thing."

Dear Elsie. Always stating the obvious.

Pat was distracted. A stranger was getting out of a little blue car by the gate. It was one of those snub-nosed Japanese things they were forever advertising on the commercial channels.

"Now, who's that?"

The newcomer was a young woman in her early thirties with glossy brown shoulder-length hair and a healthy outdoor tan. She was dressed in a crisp fifties-looking cotton shirt dress in dove grey. As she turned, the sun caught a discreet cross pinned to her lapel. The churchwarden's nose twitched. It couldn't be! The bishop wouldn't do that to them – would he?

Faith Morgan looked down the path from the wicket gate. A couple of elderly ladies were standing by an evergreen bush, cataloguing her from head to foot. This was supposed to be a low-key visit – she was only investigating options, she told herself. It might lead to nothing but still, it wouldn't do to get off on the wrong foot with the locals.

The parish church of St James's in Little Worthy rose sturdy and enduring with its sunlit graveyard at its feet. According to the guidebooks, stones in the tower had been part of a church here since Saxon times. Faith felt a wash of pleasure and peace. This place of worship had served its community for nearly a thousand years. There could hardly be a greater contrast to the gritty, uncertain, challenging chaos of the urban parish she was thinking of leaving. A pang of guilt interrupted her moment of euphoria. The face of her mentor, Canon Jonathan, came to mind, fixing her with one of his wry looks. His tart comment echoed in her head: *Little Worthy, Faith? A congregation of eight – if you're lucky – with an average age of seventy; a fund-raising nightmare to crush the heart of a saint!*

Her eyes searched the roof line. Bound to be Grade I listed. Maintaining Saxon masonry couldn't be cheap. It all *seemed* in good shape. Besides, there were always the heritage funds…

The bells began another peal, and the whiff of vanilla from a nearby shrub struck her with a breath of nostalgia. She had been here more than once as a child with Ruth and Dad on his bell-ringing outings. Those convivial summer Sundays with the dads and their kids and the occasional mother. After church they would go to the pub across the green – still called The Hare and Hounds, she noted happily. The dads would take off their ties and swap stories while she and Ruth sat outside with their lime shandies on benches of sun-warmed wood. You can never go back, she mused, so what was she doing back here?

She rallied. There was nothing wrong with peaceful continuity. Decency deserved to be cherished too.

There was a little time yet before the service began. Faith avoided the main approach and followed a gravel path around the back of the church. A creamy cloud of ivory clematis cascaded over a grey stone wall. Beyond, a solitary pony raised its chestnut head to gaze mournfully at her from a field of weeds. Some way off squatted a group of ramshackle farm buildings.

There was a well-worn track leading from the vestry door. Through a clump of limes she glimpsed the corner of what she thought must be the vicarage.

A dark-haired young man in jeans and a rumpled striped shirt strode out of the church. He had an angular face and the coltish appearance of not having quite grown into his bones. Behind him, a distinguished-looking fifty-something clergyman in surplice and cassock filled the doorway. That must be the incumbent, Alistair Ingram, thought Faith, wondering if she should introduce herself. He called out to the retreating youth, who turned back briefly to make a dismissive pushing gesture with both hands. She was about to step forward when she registered the youth's expression: disdain, fury, and something else. Triumph? Faith turned away, embarrassed. It felt like a private matter; she shouldn't be spying. She retraced her steps and entered the church.

The transition from sunlight to cool interior blinded her briefly. In a pool of clarity, Faith saw a service sheet held out in a meaty hand. It belonged to a cheery-looking man in a red waistcoat and a moss-green tweed jacket. He was smiling at her as if they knew one another.

"Fred Partridge," he pronounced in a carrying voice.

"Churchwarden. Pleased to have you with us." He winked conspiratorially as he turned to greet a couple coming in behind her.

Faith slid into an unoccupied pew. There were twenty or so worshippers scattered about. Not a bad turnout for a small country church on the fifth Sunday in Lent. Her eyes settled on the little bent woman who had been outside as she arrived. She was arranging her hymnal and prayer book on the shelf before her with delicate, twisted hands. Her fine silver hair was folded into a thin bun secured by a network of old-fashioned two-pronged pins.

A presence blocked the light from the door. The formidable-looking lady who had been sizing her up as she arrived was standing in the aisle looking at her with speculating grey eyes. She was solid, with a healthy complexion, probably in her late sixties or early seventies, dressed in what Faith's mother would refer to as "good clothes".

"You've met my fellow churchwarden, I see," she said. She had a round face and a hint of Morningside gentility in her voice. "I'm Patricia Montesque, the other one," she stated brusquely.

Faith gave her best smile and held out her hand to have it clasped briefly in paper-dry fingers.

"I'm pleased to meet you. Faith Morgan. I'm visiting for the weekend – my sister lives locally. I have fond memories of Little Worthy. We used to come here when I was a child."

"So you like our little church?"

"Isn't it beautiful?" Faith responded warmly. "So well proportioned, and a lovely, comfortable feel about it."

They contemplated the nave together.

"That's a striking arrangement," Faith remarked, indicating the display of lilacs and ivory viburnum by the altar. It was a deliberate ploy. Pat Montesque seemed the kind who was almost certain to do the flower arrangements. She was right. The churchwarden's face relaxed into a narrow smile.

"Not one of my best, I'm afraid. I was rather rushed. But

lilacs do give a lovely block of colour." She inclined her perfectly coiffed head in a faintly regal manner. "So you've family in the area, then?"

"I was born in Winchester…"

"Winchester! Barely twenty minutes away. You're almost a native."

"Almost."

"I'm just a newcomer, of course – hardly been here twenty years!" Pat Montesque gave a hard little laugh. "Not like dear Elsie Lively there." She nodded in the direction of the silver-haired lady with the bun. "She's Little Worthy born and bred. Ran the post office for half a century. A close-knit lot, the old families – but we have a very friendly parish here," she ended firmly.

Faith remembered the post office. They had sold old-fashioned sweets: shell-shaped sherbets and Parma violets. She could almost smell the sugar. Ruth always chose liquorice; not because she particularly liked the taste, but for the way it stained her tongue black.

"So you haven't met our vicar, Alistair?"

Faith was surprised by the challenge. Pat flicked a significant look at the cross pinned to her dress. So I've been rumbled, Faith thought.

"I haven't had the pleasure," she said.

"He's a good pastor. A bit of a liberal, some thought when he first came, but he's sound enough in the essentials. And very good with the finances." Pat paused. "He's leaving us, you know."

"I had heard something of the kind," murmured Faith. To think she had meant to slip in and out with being noticed. She should have known better. Rural parishes always had a Pat Montesque.

"Mmm. A bit of a dicky heart. He looks wonderfully well, but…" Her tone implied something more.

A petite woman with smooth, long fair hair, wearing a simple cotton dress came out of the vestry.

"…decided to take early retirement," continued Pat.

The blonde had striking long-lashed blue eyes and a neat-featured prettiness that retained an element of youthful innocence, although she might have turned forty – it was hard to tell. She saw the churchwarden looking at her, and gave a little girl lost smile before leaning over a pew to exchange greetings with a young mother trying to hold a squirming toddler in her lap.

Pat turned back to Faith apparently as an afterthought. "You'll be staying for coffee after the service?" Without waiting for a response, she was gone.

Could this place feel like home? Could these people ever be her people?

Faith studied the faces around her – silver-haired Elsie; the doting mother shadowing her small determined son as he ventured out down the aisle; the ruddy-faced man with the jacket too short in the sleeve, who couldn't be anything else but an English farmer; a single black family with mother and father and a boy and a girl dressed in smart Sunday clothes. Faith's eyes drifted up into the barrelled roof. There was such comfortable familiarity about the space. Why should that make her feel guilty?

Guilt. Purpose. Being of use. From the very first, Faith had always known that she wanted to be part of some greater purpose. That desire had led her into the police force. And, for a while, she thought she had found her place: to serve and protect; to bring the guilty to account; to protect the weak. That was what had first brought her and Ben together.

Running away, Faith?

I am not.

Ben always seemed to engage life so directly; he was unflinching, so sure of himself.

She was daydreaming. She could see Ben staring her down. *Taking refuge, Faith? Never thought you were a coward.*

You know I'm not, she protested the thought.

The rhythm of the old argument circled in her mind; the argument they had recycled so many times. It had moved them further and further apart, until she had left him – Ben, her lover, her mentor, her inspiration, once.

I can't hold on to your certainties any more.

He had been so hurt. She couldn't make him understand that it wasn't about him. It had been something so personal; each step on her path to the ministry had seemed undeniable.

Her eyes came to rest on a stained-glass window panel leaning against the wall in the shadows beyond the pews. She guessed it must have been taken down on its way for repair. A glass section was cracked through and the leading twisted. The echo of the panel's shape above was boarded up. A haloed lamb stood on a stretch of gaudy emerald grass. The Victorian artist had given the lamb a smiling, enigmatic expression. The Lamb of God.

Running away from reality.

That's what he'd called it. To Ben, it had been a betrayal. And was he right? Was she seeking refuge from the world?

She looked around the congregation. These were people, individual persons, with their complicated lives, their struggles, their fears, their sins, their souls.

An intelligent, capable woman past thirty – with a degree, no less – buying into this delusion… for what? Ben always challenged her. They'd been a good team, once.

What am I doing?

Finding out.

That voice was somehow neither her own nor Ben's. God and she often spoke like that. He would enter the conversation in her brain – not exactly unexpectedly. She had a sense he'd always been there. But since she had taken this turn – embraced this risk and embarked on the ministry – the sense of a presence, of an enduring and constant friend, had grown.

Finding out. The sense of opening horizons warmed and excited her. But then, what about Ben? He had moved back to Winchester more than a year ago.

And why should that matter one way or the other? He had his world now and she had hers.

The organist finished up with a self-important chord. The

vicar was standing before them. Faith pulled her thoughts back to concentrate on the service.

Alistair Ingram took a step towards the altar draped in its Lenten purple, and the choir embarked on the Agnus Dei. Faith suppressed a smile as Pat Montesque's forceful soprano rose above the rest.

"Lamb of God,

You take away the sin of the world."

The vicar's voice was clear and impressive. Faith wondered briefly if her own lighter tones could ever carry the words so well. Then she was caught up in the familiar comfort of their meaning.

"Jesus is the Lamb of God,

Who takes away the sin of the world.

Blessed are those who are called to his supper."

Alistair Ingram spread out his arms to encompass his congregation. Sunlight, tinted by the stained glass in the window behind him, painted pastel blue and red on the white linen runner laid on top of the purple cloth.

"Amen."

He picked up the communion cup and drank.

The toddler escaped from his mother and made a break for freedom past the communion rail, his feet pattering in quick uneven steps. What perfect timing. There had to be a life metaphor in that. Faith was pondering how children brought life into a church when her ears registered the choking rasp from the direction of the altar.

Alistair Ingram was staring out at nothing, his eyes wide, his chest heaving. Faith saw in slow motion. The chalice dropped from his hands. It hit the edge of the table. Wine flowed out red over the white cloth and stained the purple black. The empty cup rolled off the altar and struck the stone flags.

Alistair Ingram was no longer standing before them. Clutching at his chest and tearing at his vestments, he sat heavily on the steps.

The mother caught her son up in her arms. She turned his head into her shoulder, covering his face. Alistair slumped sideways. Faith realized that she was standing in the aisle, then she began to run towards the chancel steps.

CHAPTER

IT STRUCK FAITH HOW DEATH is always startling, facing us with the greatest mystery: how the particular and the individual can vanish from this world so completely in a moment.

The body behind the altar was almost definitely dead. Faith knew that instinctively. The servers were standing around him as if frozen.

"Perhaps I can help," she said. "I have some first aid training."

The blonde woman with the long hair was in the way. She was sitting on the floor beside the crumpled heap of robes, holding the fallen man's hand and rocking slightly. Her hair covered her face. "It's his heart. It must be his heart!" she repeated in a small, breathy voice. "Someone call an ambulance."

"Tim's doing it," mumbled Fred Partridge. His kindly face wore the fragmented look of shock as he stared helplessly to the rear of the nave, where the black father was using his mobile to phone for an ambulance, his small daughter clinging to his coat. He was stroking her glossy hair with his free hand.

"We should try CPR. But I've never done it myself..." Fred trailed off.

"I have." Faith's voice was firm and reassuring. No time to waste; there might still be a chance. She looked at the blonde woman clutching the dead man's hand. "I need some space," she said gently.

Fred put a coaxing hand on the woman's shoulder. "Jessica... Jessica, my dear – we need to give this lady room."

Faith swayed as she knelt down. She put her hand out to catch her balance. Her fingers sank into the sodden purple cloth. She felt for a pulse. There was none. Alistair Ingram was gone. A bitter memory surged up of the last time she had struggled to resuscitate a human life. It was never pleasant. Alistair Ingram was staring at something a long way beyond her. She lowered her face to the strangely plastic skin. She registered a peculiar smell. Cleaning fluid? No. That wasn't quite right. There was something odd about his lips. She looked closer – the soft tissue was swollen, irritated. His eyelids and nostrils were red-rimmed too. The smell filled her own nostrils, undeniable and acrid. It was present in the dark spreading stain dripping down the purple cloth. She was overwhelmed by a primitive intuition that she should not try oral resuscitation. Instead, she positioned herself over Ingram's solar plexus, one hand on top of the other. She began the rhythmic compressions.

"This isn't right," she heard herself say. She met Fred's worried gaze. "I think someone should call the police."

"What are you talking about?" Pat Montesque's voice intruded from beyond the barrier of stained cloth. Her upper half came into view over the plane of the altar.

"The police? It was his heart. He had trouble with his heart. He needs a doctor, not the police."

Faith was distracted as she continued to compress Ingram's chest. Her eyes searched out the glass cruet set standing on the side table. She wanted to go over and examine it, but it wouldn't do to draw attention just yet. That wasn't her role any more.

"I am afraid he is gone, Pat," Faith said, standing up. "And I really must insist we call the police."

A siren was heard in the distance. The ambulance came. The paramedics went through the motions of trying to revive Alistair Ingram. They too noted the irritation in his mouth, and used a plastic respirator. But it was no use and they knew it. The team leader, a solid man with cautious eyes, nodded when Faith said that the police were on their way.

A uniformed policeman arrived and asked everyone to stay until they had given their names and addresses. Winchester CID was sending a detective inspector out; if everybody would please wait in the body of the church.

Winchester CID. It wouldn't be; it couldn't be…

Fred and Elsie were organizing tea and biscuits at the back of the church.

"Sugar. That's the thing for shock," said Elsie. "And tea's always a comfort."

Through the open door, they saw an unmarked car draw up outside. Faith followed Fred out towards the gate. She didn't think she would be, but perhaps she was in shock. Each step seemed delayed before it registered in her brain. The car windows were tinted so she couldn't see the driver clearly. She held her breath.

A plain clothes policeman got out of the car. He was in his late twenties, tall and sandy-haired with hazel eyes. He walked up the path towards Fred and Faith.

"I hear there's been an accident," he said calmly, flipping out his warrant card. He shook hands with Fred. He looked a little rumpled, and his nose and cheeks had a blush of sunburn. He had a grass stain on his cuff. He caught Faith's look, and pulled his jacket sleeve down.

"Playing cricket with the kids," he explained. "It being Sunday and all…" he paused, flushing. Faith couldn't help smiling at him.

"Sergeant Peter Gray, ma'am."

"Faith Morgan. But I'm just a weekend visitor – Mr Partridge here is one of the churchwardens." They walked towards the church. "Sergeant, you say?"

"Yes. The boss is just behind me."

She swivelled round. And there he was, striding up the path towards her – Ben. He hadn't changed. Six foot something, dark-haired and determined with those gem-blue eyes.

"This is Detective Inspector Shorter," introduced Sergeant Gray. "Mr Partridge and – is it Ms or Mrs? – Morgan."

"Faith!" Both Sergeant Gray and Fred Partridge registered the recognition in the voice. "I don't suppose Faith Morgan answers to either, sergeant," Ben said. Leaving the startled pair standing, he grasped Faith's elbow and steered her off the path, out of earshot.

"What the hell are you doing here?" he asked. No preamble. Abrupt as ever. It was so typical, it was almost comforting – although being alone with him was the last thing she needed. "Just had to see me, eh?" He dropped his voice, suddenly teasing, intimate.

To her irritation, her hand rose of its own accord to brush back her hair. "I was invited to look at the parish. Nothing serious – I may be thinking of moving."

Too much information. She was babbling. She waved her hand towards the church. "And then this happened."

Ben reached out and caught her wrist. She stared at her hand. His large thumb lay alongside her palm. She could feel the warmth and strength of his encircling fingers. Ben reached in his pocket and brought out a paper handkerchief. She realized that her skin was stained with blood-red wine. It must have happened when she'd steadied herself by the altar. He spat on the paper and rubbed the stain away.

"Couldn't resist touching the body, eh?"

"I had to check for a pulse."

He raised a single eyebrow and released her.

"You'll be wanting to get inside and investigate," she said.

He looked at her as though they were suddenly strangers.

"Right you are." Turning on his heel, he strode back over to where Sergeant Gray and Fred were standing.

"So, sergeant, where's the body?"

Ben straightened up from his inspection of the remains of Alistair Ingram. His eyes scanned the stained altar cloth and the floor scattered with the debris of tape and torn packaging left by the paramedics. Faith couldn't justify to herself why, but she had been pulled along in his wake. Watching him, she could almost see the filing system at work in his head. Ben had a photographic memory for these things.

"A heart attack, is it?" he said to no one in particular.

The chalice was back on the altar. A half-moon stain flared out from its pedestal.

"That's what he'd just drunk from when he was taken ill?" He leaned down to sniff at it.

"There's an odd smell to it," said Faith.

Ben looked at her without expression. She almost flinched.

"Isn't there, though? What…"

Faith crossed over to the side table.

"… do they fill it from?"

Faith gestured to the glass decanter like a magician's assistant without touching it.

He half-smiled. "Right."

Ben walked up and bent over the table with his hands behind his back. He was wearing latex gloves. Faith focused on the wine in the decanter but the light was too dim; it just looked like wine. Ben leaned in and sniffed the stopper. The position showed off his long legs and strong torso. It reminded her of other times. He tilted his head to look at her quizzically, and straightened up.

"Where have SOCO got to?"

"Scene of crime are on their way, boss," Sergeant Gray answered. "Been held up on another job."

"There's a surprise."

"Don't look at me, boss. Just one of those days. And the PC says he has all the names and addresses."

Ben glanced at the congregation sitting in a bunch halfway up the nave, watching him.

"Send them home. We'll find them later if need be."

Sergeant Gray loped off. Faith turned to follow him.

She could feel Ben's eyes on her. Without meaning to, she glanced back, turning from the waist. He was looking at the line of her back. He used to say he loved those two dimples either side of her spine just where the…

"What are the chances, eh?" he said, glancing at the altar. "The tabloids are going to love this one. Right during the Eucharist. Makes you wonder what the vicar did to annoy the big boss,"

"Now's not the time for jokes," Faith said. He met her frown with a cynical look. She knew he was trying to rile her.

"What? He's going to strike me down?"

"I should be so lucky," she murmured, keeping her voice low. Sergeant Gray was walking back up the aisle towards them. He glanced back and forth between them, obviously curious.

"Someone mentioned there's a son, sir. Don Ingram – a student at Southampton University; he may be up for the vac," he said. "Pat Montesque, she's a churchwarden, she said she'd tell him, but I wondered if you'd prefer one of us to do it?"

Ben nodded. "You do it. But clear the rest of the civilians out of here first. There's no chance of uncontaminated evidence, but we'd better go through the motions."

"Oh, and I've spoken to the bishop, sir. He's sending the rural dean down, but he can't get here for another hour."

Ben looked amused.

"And the bishop asked me to tell you, ma'am," continued the sergeant, "that if you are up to it, he and his wife would still like you to come to lunch. When you're ready."

Lunch with the bishop! It had completely slipped her mind. The plans made up to that morning seemed unsubstantial and unreal. She was going to slip into the service at Little Worthy on a little side-trip of nostalgia; go on to the bishop's house, eat lunch, exchange a bit of church gossip and tell him politely that she didn't think she'd suit a rural parish. That had been the plan, hadn't it? The safest choice…

"Thank you, sergeant. I'd better give the bishop a ring."

Where was her mobile? In her bag. Her bag; she must have left it under the pew.

She'd have to go, of course. For one thing, the bishop would need briefing on what had happened as soon as possible, and since the rural dean was held up…

Faith's head was buzzing. At least that was over. She had met Ben again and survived. She had the perfect excuse to leave gracefully. He had said he wanted all civilians out. That had been aimed at her, of course.

"How about you accompany my sergeant?" Ben's voice stopped her as she picked up her bag from beneath the pew where she had been sitting.

"I'm sorry?"

"I would be grateful, ma'am, if you would accompany my sergeant to inform Don Ingram of his father's demise," he said, with exaggerated formality. "It's only just gone noon. Since the bishop says he can wait for lunch, I'm sure the victim's son would appreciate the support of someone from the God Squad," he added crudely, walking her towards the door. She focused her fury through her eyes; if only she could singe him, just a little! He was wearing his blandest expression.

Sergeant Gray frowned at his superior, looking perplexed.

"Hasn't she mentioned, sergeant? Ms Morgan is a vicar. One of the *ordained*," Ben emphasized the word. "She's a card-carrying professional at the touchy-feely stuff.'

Sergeant Gray shrugged and walked out ahead of them. Ben stood back to let Faith pass through the door before him. She felt his breath on her ear as she walked out into the sunshine.

"Must be embarrassing for you." His voice was low. "Have a man check out while you're busy eyeing up his job. Tut-tut, Fay…"

His use of his pet name for her made her stomach flip. It caught her by surprise. His eyes were twinkling. She froze him with a look and left him barking orders at the scene of crime officers lugging their equipment up the path. Pat Montesque was holding court among a small clutch of the congregation who'd been marshalled around her.

Faith headed off down the gravel that led round the back of the church.

"This way, sergeant," she said over her shoulder. "This is the short cut to the vicarage."

They passed the grey wall with its mantle of clematis.

"Any instructions on how you want to handle this, sergeant?"

"Call me Peter." His expression was boyishly engaging. Faith couldn't help smiling back.

"If you'll call me Faith. So – Peter – no one mentioned a wife; is there one?"

"Mr Ingram was a widower. Wife died a few years back. There's just the one son."

"I think I may have seen him just before the service," said Faith slowly, visualizing the dark-haired youth in the striped shirt. She almost added "… and I suspect they may have been quarrelling," but she stopped herself. Time enough for that later, if need be.

"You've known the boss long?" Peter asked.

She looked hard at the chestnut pony still chewing away in the field of weeds.

"Some time."

Peter nodded to himself.

The overgrown path turned in front of the side door and wound through some lime trees. They came to the back door of the vicarage. Don Ingram was at the kitchen window drinking from a mug. He saw them and looked irritated. He called out through the open window.

"If you're looking for the vicar, he's at church. It is Sunday, you know."

Faith sighed. This sort of thing was never easy – however much you trained for it.

"Mr Donald Ingram?"

He nodded impatiently; a posturing boy. Peter looked to Faith.

"There's been an accident at the church," she said gently. "This is Sergeant Peter Gray and my name is Faith Morgan. Can we come in?"

Don opened the door. There was a flight of three steps down to the garden. He stood in the doorway and looked down on them.

"What accident?"

Hadn't he heard the sirens? Faith wondered.

"I am afraid your father was taken ill during the service," she said. "I was there. It looked like a heart attack…"

Peter took over. "I am sorry to have to inform you, sir, but your father has passed away." He handed Don his card.

Don's face didn't change. They were only words after all.

"I am very sorry for your loss," Faith said.

Don stepped aside. "I suppose you'd better come in, then."

As she followed Peter in, Faith noticed a pretty Georgian salt box with satinwood banding hanging behind the door. The lid was open. It had been converted into a key store. That's a shame, she thought. But then, who needs that much salt these days?

It was a large kitchen. The country-style fitted cabinets stood well back from a massive scrubbed pine table.

"Should I offer you coffee or something?" Don said, looking at Peter's card.

"Shall I make some?" offered Faith. What was it about making tea and coffee in a crisis?

"If you don't mind, sir," Peter said, producing a form from the document case he carried. "There are just a few details…"

Date of birth, place of birth, the leaflet on *Sudden Death* – Faith knew the routine too well. The tramlines officialdom imposed to cross the unknowable mystery of death.

"Where is he?" Don asked, staring out of the window once more, his back to them.

"He's being taken to the Winchester Royal." Peter's tone was professionally inoffensive. "The churchwarden, Mr Partridge, is with him – and another church member. A Mrs Jessica Rose."

"Of course!" Don snorted, then paused. "Was… Were they there with him when he…"

"We all were," Faith responded, her heart going out to him. "Well, not Sergeant Gray. Your father was taken ill very suddenly during the service. It was very quick."

Don took a deep breath. He looked particularly young for a moment.

"I'd better get to the hospital, then."

"We can get someone to take you. Would you like us to fetch someone? Someone to be with you?" Faith asked.

"One of those old church biddies you mean? No!" He paused again, and turned to them. "No. I'll call a friend…" The words dried up and his mouth twisted. "We can make our own way to the hospital. I have a car."

He swung about abruptly. Faith watched him silhouetted against the window, his mobile to his ear.

"Hi. It's me. Look. Something's happened. Can you come over? Bad? Yeah. You could say that." A long pause. "Dad's dead… OK."

He put the phone down and leaned with both hands on the counter, arms rigid from the shoulder. His head dropped down.

Faith was overwhelmed with compassion. It propelled her across the room. She put a hand on his shoulder. He wasn't crying. She felt as much as heard his shallow breathing. He didn't respond for a few seconds. Then he shook her off.

"I'm all right," he said, straightening up. He glanced at her with a half-apologetic side look, and tossed his head.

"You can leave. I'll be fine. My friend's coming over."

He walked ahead of them to the front door.

The kitchen door led into a spacious hall; Georgian, with high-ceilinged rooms opening off it. The place was better kept and decorated than Faith would have expected for a vicarage. The hall floor was a wide expanse of polished parquet. A couple of modern works of art hung in handsome gilt frames against crimson walls. Possibly originals. Faith glimpsed a front room through a half-opened door. There was a beautiful Persian rug on the floor and a Bang & Olufsen sound system.

Peter broke the silence.

"We'll be in touch," he said. "You have my card. The senior investigating officer in charge of the case is Detective Inspector Shorter. If you have any queries, just give me a ring. And if you want to talk to someone, these are the contact details for the local Victim Support." He held out another card. "I've written the case number on the back."

Don stared at the oblong of cardboard between his fingers.

"But this is a crime number. You said my father had a heart attack," he said numbly.

"It's just routine," Faith heard herself saying. "It was a sudden death. Besides, every time the police are called there's always a number."

She thought of the inflammation in Alistair Ingram's mouth and the peculiar smell. It probably wasn't routine. Why lie? Because a twenty-year-old who had just lost his last close family member had enough to deal with. The mysteries surrounding the manner of the death would keep. After all, she was a civilian now. She didn't need to know any better. She looked at Peter. He was watching Don.

"I should like to come back and check on you later, if I may?" she said.

Don only half-acknowledged her with an uneasy glance.

"Are you sure you don't want someone to wait with you?" she asked again. Don Ingram was pale but he seemed calm enough. "Just until your friend comes. I can stay if…"

"No."

He shut the door on them.

They stood outside a moment contemplating the green door with its polished knocker. They walked down the drive.

"What sort of salary does a vicar get these days?" asked Peter casually.

"Not that much. Mr Ingram must have had a private income."

The drive led out onto the village green.

"Suppose the son will inherit…" Peter said.

They turned right to follow the road that looped back to the church.

"You handled yourself like a pro," Peter glanced down at her. "Done much of this sort of thing, have you?"

Faith suppressed a smile. His curiosity was palpable.

"Actually, I was a pro once," she admitted. "Well, almost – in a previous life. I trained at Hendon. I was in the police for nearly four years."

"That's where you met the boss."

She nodded.

"Aaah!" he said, drawing out the word into two syllables.

"Ah?"

"I'm saying nothing." He grinned sideways at her. She had to laugh.

"I'll have none of your cheek, young man. Remember, I'm ordained," she mimicked the way Ben had emphasized the word. "You're supposed to respect the likes of me."

"I already do, Faith," he answered.

They walked on in silence, at ease in each other's company. They were almost back at the church gate. She could see the sky-blue bonnet of her car hemmed in and incongruous among the various police vehicles. Thankfully the police personnel all seemed occupied in the church.

Peter's phone rang.

"Excuse me," he said, and stopped to answer it.

Faith walked off a few paces to give him privacy. She wondered if she should just get into her car and leave. It would take twenty minutes to get to the bishop's house. She looked at her watch. Amazingly she might actually get there soon after one, not much later than originally intended.

Just as she was making up her mind to pantomime her

goodbyes, he rang off.

"That was the boss," Peter said, deadpan. "He told me not to forget to collect your contact details. He may need to talk to you again."

CHAPTER

3

"IT IS VERY BEAUTIFUL, OF COURSE, but we need rain," said the bishop. The new leaves of the stately elm standing across the lawn below looked dusty. "The seasons seem increasingly off balance of late. Consequences. It is time our society faced the consequences of our self-indulgence." He sighed and turned away from the high window where he had been showing Faith the charming view of old Winchester.

Bishop Anthony Beech was a tall man in his mid-sixties with a healthy tan and a slight stoop. His almost tawny eyes were round and bright.

"I am so glad you felt up to coming to see us." He bobbed his head twice to emphasize his sincerity. "So glad."

They stood in a well-proportioned space flooded with light from three tall windows. The middle of the room was dominated by a vast, antique mahogany table surrounded by a set of ten chairs with high, carved backs. One end of the table's rich dark surface was set out with an assortment of plates; battered old favourites that might have been bought at a charity shop. Bishop Anthony steered Faith towards a chair with a hand on her shoulder blade.

"I am shocked. For Alistair Ingram to go so suddenly, during the very rite itself… And then the police investigation…" Words failed him.

Faith felt sorry for him and even a little guilty. She had been the one to sound the alarm.

"I am afraid the police had to be called."

The bishop gave her a sober, direct look.

"You are sure?"

"I'm afraid I am."

They contemplated the implication lying between them.

Alison Beech, a small woman with a colourless complexion and nondescript pale hair secured flat against her neat skull, came into the room carrying a basket of baked potatoes. Through the open door came the sound of a man's voice holding forth in the next room.

"But that's what I'm trying to tell you – without a secure commitment of some kind, the whole enterprise…" To Faith's ears, the voice had a note of desperation to it.

The bishop's wife closed the door softly.

"Our son, Simon," she said. "Such an unexpected treat. He's just turned up from Africa."

"He runs an irrigation project in Tanzania," explained the bishop.

His wife placed the basket on the table. "We don't get to see him and Celia that much."

"Celia?" asked Faith. Her hostess's eyes were sad.

"His wife – she stayed back this trip. No children, but they're such a good team. I'd introduce you, but he's a bit fraught," Mrs Beech said, with an apologetic grimace.

"Funding difficulties," explained her husband. "His project may have to fold."

"Oh dear," said Faith sympathetically. She could feel their parental concern.

"Yes," the bishop's wife agreed quickly. "Simon does work so very hard. But enough of that. What about this horrid business?" Mrs Beech put out a hand towards Faith. "Poor Mr Ingram. We knew he had trouble with his heart – that's why he had decided to take early retirement, wasn't it, Bishop?" She addressed her husband, making the title sound almost cozy. "And now to go

just like that, when he had hardly a few weeks left in the parish."
She shook her head. "Oh please, do sit."

The food was simple. Salads of iceberg lettuce and tomato
and a selection of cold meats laid out in a decorative spiral on a
carved African wooden platter. Bishop Anthony bowed his head
and recited a simple prayer of thanks for the food in front of
them.

"It must have been horrible for you, Faith." Mrs Beech's pale
eyes widened in sympathy. "He became ill during the service?"

Faith glanced at Bishop Anthony, unsure how to respond.
Fortunately, Mrs Beech took her hesitation for distress.

"Horrible." The corners of her mouth turned down in almost
exaggerated sorrow. "And his poor son! He's already lost his
mother to cancer, and now this. Dreadful! Quite dreadful."

"When did Don's mother die?" asked Faith, thinking of the
vicarage. There had been no obvious trace of a woman's presence
in the decor.

"Eight years or so ago. He would only have been twelve at the
time. What tragedy that boy has suffered."

"It was his wife's illness and death that brought Alistair to
us," explained the bishop. "He was a money man in the City.
Joined a bereavement group at St Martin-in-the-Fields and ended
up training for the ministry. A great asset to the church. He will
be sorely missed."

"Of course, he had been having a terrible time," chimed in
Mrs Beech. "Not happy. No…" She was searching the table and
missed her husband's warning look. "All that bother with the
neighbouring farmer. Chutney?" she asked, offering a jar to Faith.
"It's home-made."

"Reverend Ingram had been having trouble with a neighbour?"
asked Faith.

Bishop Anthony looked uncomfortable. When he'd suggested
that Faith take a look at Little Worthy, he hadn't mentioned any
disputes.

"A little local difficulty over a covenanted field," he said, and put a forkful of salad in his mouth.

"A bit more than that, dear, wasn't there?" said his wife. "Didn't Luke tell us that the poor man found a load of manure dumped halfway down the vicarage drive in the middle of the night? Luke McIvor," she explained to Faith. "Agent for the diocesan lands."

"That sounds unpleasant," said Faith. "Were there other incidents?"

The bishop shifted in his chair. "Not exactly incidents. Well, these rural parishes, you know…"

"There has been a long-running dispute between the family that farms the land that runs alongside the church and the vicarage – and the incumbent at Little Worthy." Faith wondered if Alison Beech was short-sighted. She certainly didn't seem to be aware of her husband's expression as she rattled on. "Some say it goes back centuries."

Faith thought of the pony she'd seen in the field beside the church, scratching around in the field of weeds. So Alistair Ingram had more reasons for taking early retirement than just his dodgy heart. She filed the thought away. It was too easy to get carried away with speculation. She wondered how Ben's information gathering was progressing. The bishop was staring at a spot just above his plate. His expression was poignant. Her conscience wrestled between curiosity and compassion. Compassion won. Faith helped herself to a rolled slice of ham.

"What a remarkable platter," she commented.

Mrs Beech's face lit up.

"It's Bantu. From Tanzania. We were out there for – oh, nearly twelve years." She looked nostalgically at the platter. "Missionary work is something of a family line, as you may have gathered, Faith. Those were very happy years."

Both the Beeches' faces were bright with remembered affection.

"We miss our friends there," said the bishop, simply. "Our people – our congregation – such energy; so simple and wholehearted in their belief. Such a young people, and yet utterly trusting in the Lord."

"And your son still works there?" asked Faith.

"Yes," said the bishop, looking down at his plate. "He runs WATA."

"It stands for Winchester Aid for Tanzanian Agriculture," he explained. "But sadly, the finances aren't good. It's always the same. The hardest part is raising the money."

"So we haven't abandoned them entirely," Alison said, meeting her husband's eye over the platter. There was a note in her voice that made Faith wonder whether it was a phrase that had been often repeated. "More salad, Faith?"

"Thank you," said Faith, helping herself to seconds from the proffered bowl. "These tomatoes are wonderfully flavoursome." Bishop Anthony smiled. "You don't grow them yourself?" she asked.

"No. Sadly I don't have the time, but I do like to go and watch them grow."

Faith thought for a moment that he was joking, but the bishop's expression was sincere.

"Anthony is a great supporter of ACORN; it's his pet project. And I encourage him," declared Mrs Beech. "He needs a peaceful place to get away from all the pressures of this job. And the farm's only fifteen minutes down the road."

"ACORN?" echoed Faith.

"Agricultural Community for Organic Renewables Now – I think that's what it stands for; I can never quite remember," said Alison. "It's run by some wonderful young people. Anthony negotiated their use of diocesan land a few years back and they have done marvellous things. We get all our vegetables from them."

"It is a sustainable development project," the bishop took over, his commitment clear. "It is about minimizing human impact and living in harmony with nature. Most inspiring. As Alison says, they are an excellent group of young people. Enthusiastic and caring of one another…"

"Wholehearted," said Faith, smiling.

"Yes. Wholehearted and Christian too. They live in and out of their faith. They give me such hope for the new generation."

"And speaking of the new generation…" Mrs Beech pinned Faith with a look. "Anthony mentioned that you have family in the area, Faith."

"My elder sister lives near Little Worthy. We grew up here in Winchester."

"So you're thinking of coming home?" suggested Mrs Beech.

Bishop Anthony was listening with a benignly neutral expression. Faith was uncomfortable. She didn't want to mislead him. It was flattering that he should be interested in attracting her to the diocese, but she wasn't clear in her own mind what she was doing here. For the last few months she had been restless. She had a sense that she was being nudged in some new direction – perhaps, she hoped, even by God – but she wasn't clear yet what that direction was. How should she answer?

Just speak the truth.

"I think I am ready for a new challenge," she said.

After lunch, Mrs Beech suggested they head down to the hospital to check on Reverend Ingram's son. The hospital was eerily quiet when they arrived. Faith had to remind herself that it was Sunday afternoon.

Alison was thoughtful. She caught Faith watching her.

"Hospitals!" she said. "The time I've spent!"

Faith was intrigued. Alison looked a little embarrassed.

"It's just that we had quite a time with our Simon when he was young. We were out in Africa, upcountry, and he became very ill, poor little boy. It was quite a do. I flew back with him to England. Anthony and I were separated for months. But we all survived in the end. This way, I think."

Mrs Beech found a porter who led them to an anonymous corridor where they discovered a bored constable standing a few yards from a line of tubular steel chairs. On one of the chairs Don Ingram sat looking at the grey linoleum between his feet.

"Is that the boy?" Alison asked in a whisper. Don raised his head and looked at them.

"Faith Morgan. You remember me from earlier? This is Mrs Beech, the bishop's wife."

Alison captured one of the youth's hands in both of hers.

"Donald, I am so very, very sorry," she said with great sincerity. "It is a dreadful loss. Your father was a good, faithful man." She paused, gazing compassionately into his face. "Would you like us to pray together?"

Don looked revolted. Faith winced internally. She could see that he was not one of the young who prayed – at least, perhaps not publicly on demand.

"Why are you alone?" she intervened. "Has anyone come to tell you what's happening? Have you seen your father?"

"They won't let me see him," Don said dully.

"What? Won't let you see him? But why ever not?" Mrs Beech looked up and down the corridor. She homed in on the constable and shepherded him a few yards away.

Don turned accusingly on Faith. "The police think it's murder."

She met his stare.

"Murder?" she repeated cautiously.

"Poisoned by the wine – the communion wine." He snorted. "Written off by the rite. There's irony!" He gave a hard little laugh.

She covered his hand with hers. His long fingers were cool.

"But your father believed in it."

"Yes." He nodded, sobered. "Yes. He did."

His eyes wandered away down the blank corridor.

"This is weird."

"Yes. It is."

Don resumed his study of the floor between his feet. Faith looked down at the back of his head. His hair was thick. He had little lamb curls at the nape of his neck.

"I thought you had rung your friend," she said.

Don slid her a look then glanced away down the corridor.

"He's here. He's just getting coffee."

"That sounds like a good idea. Perhaps I'll go see if I can find someone."

"Follow the blue line on the wall in that direction," he indicated briefly, with a slight toss of his head.

Follow the blue line. The corridor turned.

She almost collided with a slim young man with wise, watchful brown eyes and floppy blond-brown hair, holding two cups of coffee.

"Sean!" Faith's mind flashed to Ruth, terrified that something awful had happened to her. This day couldn't be getting any worse, could it?

"Aunt Faith." Sean had always been unflappable, but surely he wouldn't be this calm if something had happened to her sister. He seemed pleased to see her.

"Sorry I missed you last night. I was out." Holding the coffees to one side, her nephew pecked her on the cheek.

"What *are* you doing here?"

Sean's face turned solemn.

"Supporting a friend. His father's just died."

"You know Don Ingram?"

Sean looked surprised.

"You remember Don. We were on the cricket team at school? We're at uni together?"

"That Don?" Faith had heard the name, but she'd never really been around enough to notice Sean's friends. Then she wondered if Don had recognized her. If so, why hadn't he said anything?

The coincidences were unsettling. It was as if Winchester was reclaiming her. Sean gave her a lazy smile.

"Good to see you."

"You too. We must catch up."

He glanced down the corridor leading back to Don.

He grimaced.

"Maybe not tonight, though. I was thinking of staying in town with Dad."

Sean's father Brian had left Ruth when Sean was a baby. He was an ambitious IT salesman who had traded up to a wife whom he considered more suitable to his career path. Brian had always liked money. Faith had never thought much of him, but he was an amiable father. He and his latest wife had a townhouse in the centre of Winchester and they always welcomed Sean there.

"Perhaps you could stay with Don," she ventured.

"Don't worry, I'll look in on him," said Sean. "Are you staying around long?"

"Another day or two at least," Faith said. "We can catch up later. Maybe at your mum's."

He looked a little dubious. "These coffees are getting cold." He began to back away. "If you want some, the machine's just round there. Ben's there."

"Ben?"

"Yeah. He's on Don's case – how's that for weird, eh?" Sean did a neat about-turn without spilling the coffees, and disappeared.

Weird indeed. Faith felt as if she had fallen down Alice's rabbit hole – Sean appearing then disappearing down one elbow of the tubular corridor, and Ben waiting somewhere around the next bend.

The coffee machine. And there was Ben leaning against the wall talking into his mobile.

They exchanged a brief nod. He went on talking into the phone. Faith focused on getting her purse out of her bag. At last she rolled the coins into the slot. One slipped away from her. She bent over from the waist to pick it up, blood rushing to her face. As her fingers felt the coin, she realized her back was to Ben. She straightened up. Out of the corner of her eye she caught him looking away. The cup fell into the dispenser. She listened to the coffee being hosed into the plastic. Ben closed his phone.

"Black, one sugar for me."

She hesitated.

"I've got the money." He made an elaborate gesture towards his pocket.

She waved a hand and punched in the code. "I'll treat you."

Faith sipped the hot coffee in silence. It was really quite disgusting.

"Knew you couldn't stay away."

"I'm with the bishop's wife; she wanted to check on Don Ingram."

He looked down at her under his lashes, his eyes crinkling at the sides. She gave in.

"Oh, all right! I'm curious. So it's poison?"

"Not officially. We're waiting for the tests to come back – but yes. Looks like it. So much for Christian charity."

"It's such an awful thing to do."

"Murder usually is."

"You know what I mean. Right there in the midst of the communion service, so public and so, well…"

"… blasphemous?" Ben suggested, rolling his eyes. "So you don't fancy one of the congregation?"

"I can't see a committed Christian… well, to murder a man at the height of the most important part of the service? It's not just about the individual – it's a direct insult to God."

"Perhaps the murderer thought Ingram had insulted God. Struck him down – a wrath of God thing."

"In Little Worthy?" Faith said, raising her eyebrows.

He smiled down at her indulgently. "How did you ever survive four years in the force?"

"Just because I don't see criminals and psychopaths at every turn! I see people as they are."

"You keep on thinking that." He lobbed his empty cup into the bin and half-turned away. He hesitated.

"Heard you might be moving back this way," he said.

How could he have heard? They hadn't spoken for nearly a year. At first there had been phone calls – but it just seemed too painful. They had tapered off to email and then the occasional postcard. He glanced at her. His eyes were such a vivid blue.

"Sammy told me."

Sammy. Of course. Sammy was the wife of Ben's first chief inspector, Eric. She was their last remaining link.

"Saw Sean just now." Ben interrupted her thoughts. "Looks like your family are well embedded in this case. You staying with Ruth?"

"For a few days at least."

"And do I infer from your pastoral interest in young Ingram that I shall be seeing you around Little Worthy – for a few days at least?"

Faith didn't want to answer that.

He leaned towards her with a grin. "You can be my spy in the camp," he said, conspiratorially.

Faith watched him walk away. *I'm not your anything any more*, she thought, and was annoyed with herself because that sounded wistful. *And I certainly won't be your spy*, she assured herself firmly. Still, the prospect of divided loyalties lingered indigestibly.

Then her mind returned to the question flashing in neon over them all. Who in Little Worthy could be mad enough to poison communion wine?

CHAPTER

"I'M WORRIED ABOUT HER." Ruth stood at the window of her compact kitchen, peeling onions under running water at the sink. She had moved into the house as a new build. She said she liked the convenience – everything at arm's length. The kitchen reminded Faith of a doll's house. She was slightly nervous of leaning against the fittings in case, being fully grown, she broke something. She was only a couple of inches taller, but at five foot four and slight with it, Ruth had always made much of her smaller size.

"She seems fine to me," Faith responded. Ruth worried about Mum perpetually. Faith took a sip of the wine she had brought. She'd stopped off to pick it up at the twenty-four-hour place on the roundabout on her way back from the hospital. Sunday trading. She supposed she ought to feel guilty, but there was no getting around it; it was convenient.

"I want her to move back here, where I can keep an eye on her." Ruth wiped her eyes with the back of her hand. The water treatment wasn't working too well. Her eyes were tearing.

"She has her own life; her own friends. She likes it in Birmingham," Faith responded soothingly. After their father died, five years ago, Mum had chosen to move back to Birmingham. Marianne Morgan had grown up in the city and she still thought of it as home, even though she had brought her daughters up in Winchester.

Ruth was Faith's elder by four years. Unlike Faith, who had gone off to college, she had married young and had Sean. She prided herself on her superior sensitivity and expertise in family matters. To her mind their mother, being now in her seventies, was in that phase in her life when she needed to be "looked after". Faith never thought of her mother like that. In her eyes, Marianne was still the humorous, capable, self-reliant woman she had always been. They enjoyed each other's company and Faith had been pleased to find a post in a neighbouring parish, near to her mother, for her first curacy.

Despite her red eyes, Ruth cast her one of her superior big sister looks.

"I know you only live down the road, but you're so busy with the parish. I ring her every day. I don't think she's coping."

Here it comes, thought Faith.

The phone rang in the hall.

Ruth was scrabbling around for a tea towel to dry her hands. Faith went into the hall, grateful for the interruption.

"I'll get it," she said as she picked up the receiver. "Hello."

"Just the woman I was looking for," the familiar voice said in her ear.

"Ben."

In the kitchen, Ruth turned away. She had a smug look on her face.

"The one and only." He sounded as if he had been drinking. Faith looked at her own glass on the hall table. Who was she to judge?

"Thought you'd like to know. Had the prelims back. Looks like someone spiked the wine with pesticide."

"You sure? It couldn't be a mistake? Contamination at the bottling plant..." As she spoke she knew how ridiculous it sounded. Ben's silence at the other end spoke volumes. "I know, I know. Not likely."

"Not unless something's wrong with the phones and

congregations up and down the land have been suffering fatalities without mentioning it," he said. She felt the corners of her mouth curving upwards, smiling against her will. The pause lengthened between them.

"Found out anything I should know about?"

The question jolted her back to reality. She was balancing over a rift: Ben and his investigation on one side, and the church in the persons of the bishop and the congregation of St James's of Little Worthy on the other. She thought of what the bishop's wife had said about the dispute with the neighbouring farmer. She felt uncomfortable about repeating it. She wasn't sure of her facts. She wasn't in the police force any more. It wasn't her job to spy for Ben.

"Nothing worth reporting."

"Right." His tone was sarcastic. He knew her too well. "So what is it that's not worth reporting? Come on. What did his holiness give up?"

"Don't. Bishop Anthony's a good man. He deserves respect."

"All right. I'm sorry." He sounded contrite. He'd always kept doing that; just when she was convinced he was impossible, he'd surprise her.

"So what did he say?" Ben prompted.

He never gave up.

"It was nothing. There was just a mention that whoever farms next to the vicarage was upset about some church covenants he thought were restricting his use of the land. Just normal country stuff."

"Covenants?" Ben queried.

"I'm not sure; I assume the land once belonged to the church and it was sold with a covenant on it restricting the uses the land could be put to," Faith explained. "Perhaps the farmer's not allowed to build on it. I don't know. The bishop didn't go into details. It wasn't a big deal."

"So why did it come up?"

"The bishop's wife suggested that Alastair Ingram had been

a bit stressed."

"Suicide?"

"No! Nothing like that."

"So what? Poison pen letters, shouting matches, vandalism…"
He stopped. Sometimes Ben's intuition was unnerving.
"Vandalism?"

"Just some manure dumped in the vicarage driveway one
night. Childishness."

Ben was silent at the other end of the phone.

"There's no reason to think it connects," Faith protested.

"I'd better leave you to your evening. Supper with sister?" he
asked cheekily. "Remember me to Ruth." That was sarcasm. He
had never really taken to Ruth – despite her being rather struck
by him.

"What are you…?" Faith began, but he had already rung off.
She put the receiver back in the cradle with a snap. Ben always
had to be unsettling.

In the kitchen, Ruth was stirring hamburger ingredients in a
large steel bowl.

"So that was Ben," her big sister said.

Faith didn't really want to talk about it.

"I saw Sean at the hospital," she said instead. "He was with
Don Ingram, the murdered vicar's son."

Ruth stirred vigorously. "They're friends. Been friends since
school and now they're at uni together."

"That's good. Uni can be a lonely place, everyone trying to
impress each other."

Ruth plonked the bowl down on the surface and dug her
hands into the mixture, bringing out a fistful of ground mince.
She rolled it between her hands, patting it into shape. "I hardly
see him at all anymore," she said. "He used to ring twice a week,
but now I'm lucky if we snatch five minutes in a month. Usually
he doesn't even pick up!"

"You know what it's like," said Faith. "There are lots of
distractions."

Ruth slapped the half-formed hamburger on the counter. "Mmm. But back to Ben."

Oh Lord!

"So?" Ruth lay her freshly formed hamburger into the frying pan she had heating on the stove. "Ben. He's here; you could move here. Have you finally come to your senses?"

She wore a wry smile, but Faith knew that Ruth had never really understood why she broke up with Ben. In Ruth's mind, Ben was a class-A catch: strong, decisive, handsome, a proper man. Ruth had never really got over being abandoned by Brian, either. For her little sister to throw away a catch like Ben – well, it was not only wasteful, but provoking. Faith understood that much.

"Ruth, we don't fit," she said. Her sister looked a little impatient. Faith ploughed on. "We live in different worlds. He has his life; I have mine."

"You used to be in the same world."

Ruth was an atheist. She didn't like imponderables. Faith sipped her wine, but didn't want to get into an argument.

Ruth flipped the hamburger, sending up a splash of hot fat that stung her on the inside of the wrist. She sucked it impatiently.

"And I haven't decided whether or not I'm moving yet. I don't know whether I fit back here, either." Faith fetched a piece of kitchen towel. She ran it under the cold water tap and pressed it to the round red burn on her sister's wrist. "This mad tragedy at Little Worthy – well, it's not really my business, and I don't see there's any reason why I should have anything much more to do with it."

"You're just hanging around?"

"I'm visiting my loving sister. I don't need any other reason." Faith banged her forehead softly against her sister's thick hair.

"Huh!" Ruth snorted through her nose and gave the hamburger a smack with her spatula.

Faith went to bed early. Relaxed by a couple of glasses of wine, she drifted off in the narrow bed in the small spare room, for once oblivious to Ruth's collection of Cabbage Patch dolls looming grotesquely from the shelf running around the dado rail.

In the depths of the night, she stood again next to the stained altar cloth and peered down at Alistair Ingram's crumpled form. Her head was buzzing. There was coloured light streaming in through the stained-glass window. Emerald green and yellow. Bishop Anthony stepped over the vicar's body. "Here," he said. "Take it." She looked down at his hands and saw he was holding out the chalice. It was sticky with spilled wine. Up in the window, the stained-glass lamb smiled enigmatically. Its expression somehow reminded her of Ben. She gasped for air.

"Phone!" She was being shaken. "Faith, wake up. The phone."

She opened her eyes and saw Ruth.

"It's past eight and the bishop is on the phone for you."

Faith sat up, rubbing her eyes with the heels of her hands. "Can I call him back?"

"He's waited this long. I'd take it," said her sister unhelpfully, leaving the room. "I've got to get to work."

Faith slipped her feet into her pink Percy Pig slippers and padded to the phone. On her way down the stairs she stretched in an exaggerated yawn, hoping to wake up her vocal cords. Bishop Anthony probably never slept in.

"I am sorry to ring first thing," said the bishop briskly, "but I was hoping to have a word with you about Little Worthy."

Faith stared at the phone. Was she still dreaming?

"I've had a chat with Bishop Michael and he says they can spare you." Bishop Michael was her bishop back in Birmingham. "I was hoping that you might stay with us a while and fill in at Little Worthy – for the time being at least. This tragedy. The congregation need support, all the more so in the run-up to Easter. Since you happened to be... Are you there?"

"Yes. Yes. I'm sorry. Just it is all rather sudden."

"Indeed." Bishop Anthony was respectfully quiet for a moment.

"But of course, I am happy to do anything I can to help," Faith said.

"Excellent! We are lucky to have you. Perhaps you can come and have a chat. Today? Ten-ish? Would that suit you?"

Faith looked at her wrist. Her watch was upstairs. What time was it? She felt dizzy, disorientated.

"Fine," she heard herself say.

"I'll see you at ten," Bishop Anthony said, and rang off.

She put the phone down and stared at it. What had she just agreed to? She'd spoken on instinct. She couldn't take it back.

Was I supposed to do that?

Let's find out.

Bishop Anthony's secretary was a dumpy woman with iron-grey hair who looked as if she found life a trial. She ushered Faith through a heavy oak door and retreated to answer a ringing phone.

The room was lined floor to ceiling with bookcases crammed with files and leather-bound journals and books. The one uncluttered space was the upper half of the chimney breast. Beneath it, an ugly electric bar heater glowed within the shell of a Georgian fireplace. Bishop Anthony sat with his back to the window, behind an over-sized desk. He was not alone. A slim young clergyman with an intense expression and receding hair cropped close was sitting in one of a pair of green wing armchairs upholstered in a durable acrylic bouclé.

"Faith – so glad you could join us." Bishop Anthony emerged from behind the solid mass of his desk to greet her with warmth. "Let me introduce you to George Casey, our diocesan press officer."

Casey had clear eyes and the even tan of a fair-weather sailor. He rocked out of the upholstered depths to grasp the tips of her fingers in a brief, snapping grip before dropping back into his seat as if to indicate that there were more pressing matters at hand.

"George was hoping to catch a word with you about the situation at Little Worthy," explained the bishop as he waved Faith into the second chair.

"I've no need to emphasize, I am sure, the negative implications for the diocese if this story should get away from us, Miss Morgan." Casey's delivery was clipped.

The chair was roomier than Faith had anticipated. It engulfed her. The seat seemed to be on an incline, tipping her weight backwards into the mossy depths. Her view of the room was reduced to a vignette of the looming press officer, and a distant Bishop Anthony behind his desk. Faith felt at a distinct disadvantage.

"Situations like this – they are delicate." George Casey pinned her with his intensity, leaning forward, his forearms on his knees.

Situations like this? Faith echoed silently. Were murders so common? She attempted to shuffle forward in the seat to gain a bit of height. George Casey frowned impatiently at her squirming.

"The key is controlling the flow of information," he stated. "A couple of the local reporters have been sniffing around." He glanced at Bishop Anthony. "But I am handling that," he assured him.

"We've issued a statement to the local papers," the bishop explained. Again his press officer cut in. The man had no manners, thought Faith crossly.

"Heart attack. Terrible tragedy. The bishop requests that the privacy of family and congregation be respected in this time of sorrow – that sort of thing," George Casey rattled off. "I'll email you a copy, so you can familiarize yourself."

Faith could feel her mouth setting into a disapproving line. She tried to relax. She was here to learn how to be of use. It wasn't her place to take offence at the social skills, or lack of them, of the diocesan press officer.

There was a sound behind her. The study door had opened.

"Sorry. Didn't realize you had people in." A male voice spoke rapidly. By the expression on Bishop Anthony's face, the voice's owner was familiar to him. Faith leaned out of her confinement, craning her neck as far as seemed polite to get a view of the newcomer, but the chair's wing cut off the last third of the door. She smiled warmly in the general direction, in case the visitor had a view of the tip of her profile.

"Simon…" Bishop Anthony began. In the way of families, his son did not wait for him to finish.

"The flying tomato needs a tune-up; it's making a terrible racket. I was going to take it to that fellow off St Cross Road. Do you know if he's still in business?"

"The man down by the hospital? I think so."

"Thanks. I'll try him."

The door clicked shut.

"My son, Simon," explained the bishop unnecessarily. "He's getting about in my wife's old car while he's with us. It's always developing some rattle or other."

George Casey cleared his throat.

"As I was saying – in a situation such as we face now in Little Worthy, it is imperative that people – if you'll forgive a secular phrase – stay on-message."

Faith struggled to keep her expression benign. To be honest, she was a bit shocked. The man was talking as if he thought the church should emulate the media management of political spin doctors. She glanced at Bishop Anthony – was he in agreement with this?

"All it takes is an overly chatty parishioner or the passing opinion of some retired canon and…" The press officer made an exclamatory shape with his lean fingers. "I don't want to seem alarmist, but a story like this can affect the way people perceive the diocese for years."

Behind his desk, Bishop Anthony issued a soft "tut". Casey stared at Faith accusingly as if hers were just the sort of passing opinions he was hoping to silence.

With an inelegant lurch, Faith extricated herself from the depths of the seat to perch on the edge of it.

"These chairs are a bit all-embracing, aren't they?" she remarked cheerfully. Bishop Anthony looked faintly startled.

"Mr Casey, I appreciate your desire to provide the bishop with a professional service," she said, hoping she sounded more polite than she felt. "But a clergyman of this diocese has been murdered right in the middle of a Eucharist – a traumatic and tragic event which was witnessed by twenty or more members of his congregation." She appealed to Bishop Anthony. "I don't see how the diocese – or anyone – can hope to control what people say about that event, or even if we should."

George Casey opened his mouth to respond.

"Naturally, the press will be aware of the police investigation," Bishop Anthony intervened diplomatically.

"Indeed," agreed Casey curtly, "and of course, we have no control over what leaks there may be from police."

Really, the man was intolerable.

"I can assure you that the senior investigating officer in charge will be just as keen as you to keep press involvement to a minimum," snapped Faith.

"You know him?" Casey's eyes brightened. "That could be useful." His expression shifted to thoughtful. "Of course, we can always stick to the 'can't comment due to ongoing investigation' line…"

Anthony Beech appraised Faith with a glance.

"Sadly, we have no time to continue this discussion today," he said firmly, rising. "I must have a brief word with Faith before I leave for my next appointment. Thank you so much for coming in, George." Faith watched, impressed, as he shepherded his press officer to the door. "I am glad you two have had an opportunity to meet."

The bishop watched the pair of them in a fatherly manner as they exchanged a perfunctory handshake. "I can assure you, George, that with her background, Faith is better aware than most of the media implications of our…" – the bishop hesitated briefly – "… situation."

Casey produced a stack of business cards and thrust them at Faith. "If you could make sure any press contacts go through me," he said, "and do check your emails for the approved statement." He smiled thinly and left.

Bishop Anthony returned to his desk.

"You'll want to run up to Birmingham to fetch some things, I know, but the churchwardens are hoping you'll be able to join them. They're meeting in Little Worthy church hall at noon."

Fifteen minutes later, Faith sat in her car outside the diocesan offices rearranging the Reverend Casey's cards in her handbag. She was startled by Bishop Anthony's efficiency. In less than twenty-four hours he had spoken to her bishop and her vicar, and arranged for her to take temporary charge at St James's, Little Worthy. He must have started phoning last night, she thought.

Her life had been hijacked.

Just think how Alistair Ingram must feel.

Now that was inappropriate, she scolded herself. Ben was a bad influence on her.

She sat in the reassuringly familiar comfort of her little blue car, took a deep breath and wondered what she should do next.

The cure of souls of the parish of St James's was in her care.

At least temporarily.

She had over an hour before the church hall meeting.

There are others who need you.

She wasn't sure the voice was correct. Don Ingram seemed quite happy to be on his own.

It can't hurt to try.

She put the car in gear and set off in the direction of Little Worthy.

CHAPTER

5

"IT'S YOU!" DON GREETED HER as he opened the front door.

"It is," responded Faith, a little surprised to find him so friendly after their conversation at the hospital the day before.

"Come in," he said, sweeping a hand out in an exaggerated gesture of welcome. He wore a crisp white shirt loose over tapered black jeans that fitted him well. He was a good-looking boy. "Come to advise me on funeral arrangements?" His tone was unsettlingly jaunty.

"Can I help? Do you need help in finding a funeral director, or..."

"Already sorted." He cut her off mid-sentence, ushering her towards the kitchen as if they were friends. "Spoke to them first thing. Business of death all under control."

"I just thought I should drop in to see how you are... and," Faith took a deep breath, "warn you that the bishop has asked me to stay on a while."

Don stopped in his tracks.

"I am going to be helping out at Little Worthy."

He stared at her, his eyes like ice.

"Filling the former incumbent's shoes – so soon?" he asked, his voice smooth and sarcastic. Then his face became human again. "Don't worry." He backed away from her, gesturing that she should follow. "Coffee?"

A sheaf of cards lay fanned out on the table.

"These have already started coming in." He flipped open one of the condolence cards. "*Condolences on your father's passing,*" he read. "Haven't the faintest who sent it." He made a disgusted noise in his throat. "His passing! That's Little Worthy for you; must keep up the façade!" He tossed the card back on the pile.

"How are you doing?" Faith was concerned. "You haven't spent the night here on your own, have you?"

"I'm fine," he said. He looked at her almost indulgently. "Sean came over. He's gone off already. Had an interview somewhere this morning, but we fitted in the phone call to the funeral director before he left. We're aiming for Friday. Cappuccino?"

Faith watched him produce the frothy drink from an elaborate, gleaming coffee machine with much hissing of steam.

"Friday – you mean the funeral?"

"Yes. Here in the church. I suppose someone has to take it," he added, as if the thought had just occurred to him. He looked at her directly. "You free, by any chance?"

She felt absurdly honoured. It was almost as if he trusted her.

"It would be a privilege, but I'm not sure… This isn't my diocese; I would need to consult the bishop."

His face closed down. "Of course! My father's death is a church matter, after all. By the way, your policeman friend rang," he said, abruptly changing the subject. "It's confirmed. The wine was poisoned."

Her policeman friend. Just how much background had Sean been giving him about her? Don sat down opposite her across the pine expanse of the table. In full light he seemed brittle. His skin was sallow and his eyes weren't entirely focused.

"And they're releasing the body to you already?" asked Faith, slightly surprised as the words left her mouth. She'd known murder victims in the mortuary for weeks.

"The full post-mortem isn't done yet but they say I should

have Dad back – well, most of him – by Friday." He stopped suddenly.

It was the word "Dad" that tripped him up, Faith thought. He was doing so well until then.

"Is there no other family you can call?" she asked. "Someone should be here to stand alongside if nothing else."

"Stand alongside!" His snort of laughter was humourless. "Is that what family does?"

"Didn't you get on with your father?"

He shrugged, his eyes on his coffee. "He was all right. We didn't exactly sing from the same sheet." He glanced up at her. She saw his eyes were tearing. "Man of God, son of science. Different world views." He looked away again.

"You're studying physics, I think."

"You've been asking about me," he quipped.

She smiled. "And not a churchgoer."

"No." He looked up from his coffee, challenging her. "I think religion does more harm than good." He cocked his head. "Do I offend?"

"Not in the least," she responded cheerfully. "Sometimes I agree with you."

She'd startled him.

"But," she added quietly, "for me, faith is a different matter."

Don cleared his throat. "It seems your inspector has a suspect."

Faith felt a pang of anxiety. "Oh?"

"They've taken Trevor Shoesmith in for questioning. The farmer next door. Someone told the policeman about his dispute with my..." – he hesitated over the word – "...father. Not sure who."

That was quick work. But then, Ben never hung around.

Don was watching her reaction. And, to her surprise, Faith felt a little guilty. She kept her expression bland.

"Do you think this Shoesmith is a likely suspect?" she asked.

Don grimaced dismissively. "He's a loser; a loner. Doesn't talk much. I do know he's a lousy farmer. I wouldn't want to be one of his animals. RSPCA's been on to him more than once."

"You think he's unhinged?"

Don shrugged. "How should I know? We didn't socialize." He leaned across the table and picked up her empty cup. "More coffee, Nancy Drew?"

Ten minutes and another cappuccino later, she left him with her mobile number and a promise to call again in a couple of days. She wasn't sure what to make of Don. Perhaps she should ask Sean. He was an excellent judge of character.

The vicarage had one of those rare untouched nineteenth century gardens with romantic old trees and swathes of daffodils along the drive. She stopped to appreciate it for a moment. So many of these plots had gone for development; covered over by executive homes of raw brick with contrasting concrete, pocket handkerchief lawns and spindly plants in designer gravel. She sighed and breathed in the country air.

"Faith!" Through the trees, she saw Peter Gray hailing her from the field running alongside the vicarage garden. She walked over and they shook hands across the open fence.

"Fancy meeting you," she said.

"Been visiting the son? How is he?"

"A bit odd."

"Odd?" Peter lifted his ginger eyebrows in enquiry. The expression was a little comical on his open, boyish face.

"Odd. I can't quite put my finger on it. I suspect it is youthful bravado. I'm not sure that father and son got on terribly well."

"I didn't with my father when I was his age."

Faith knew she liked Peter. He was sensible. Lots of young men didn't get on with their fathers. It didn't make them murderers.

"I hear you've been questioning the farmer. Think you have a suspect?"

"Don't know about the poisoning, but he's not a good

farmer," Peter's expression darkened. "You should see this place. I'd say Trevor Shoesmith has been struggling for some time."

"He's on his own, then?"

"Yes. Just him since his parents died. Word is they ran a neat place. They must be turning in their graves."

"Poor man. Do you think he's depressive?"

"Maybe."

"What does Ben – Detective Shorter – think?"

Peter half-smiled at her slip, but she realized she'd made him uncomfortable.

"I'm sorry. I keep forgetting. You can't discuss the investigation."

Peter's face cleared. "That's all right. I trust you – the boss isn't looking forward to the story getting out. He hates journos and they're going to be all over this. He's invited Shoesmith in for questioning, but he's hoping to use the RSPCA for cover. They've been out to the animals."

Faith wondered if Ben thought he'd got his man. Would he have picked up Trevor Shoesmith if she hadn't repeated that piece of hearsay? It made her uneasy.

She realized Peter was watching her, waiting for her to speak.

"I should get going. I am expected at a meeting at the church hall," she said.

"I'm heading the same way," he replied.

They walked down together towards the village green, with the fence between them.

"Do you live locally?" she asked.

"Over in the next village. Sandra and I moved in a couple of months ago. We're still settling in."

"And you've children?"

"Two boys – Daniel and Charlie; six and four." He beamed with pride.

"You like it here?"

"It's pleasant. But we haven't found ourselves a church yet."

He slid her a side glance from under his stubby lashes. "You thinking of staying on at St James's?"

"The bishop's asked me to fill in just for now," Faith admitted.

"That's brave of you."

She smiled wryly. She didn't feel brave. She felt as if she were stumbling blindly into the unknown.

They'd reached the boundary wall facing the green. She faced him across the fence. "So perhaps I shall see you and your family here one Sunday?"

"That you may."

She left Peter to follow the stone wall down to the gate.

"And Faith…"

She turned back.

"If anything comes up," Peter tossed his head in the general direction of the church, "and you want to discuss it, feel free." He held out his card across the fence. She took it. He had written his private mobile number on it. She smiled and put it in her pocket.

The church hall was once the village school. It was a neat, single-storey stone building with "1880" chiselled over the lintel. The arched wooden door was freshly painted white in gleaming contrast to the black iron strap hinges. Well maintained, Faith thought, as she turned the heavy ring handle. The parish finances must be sound.

She stepped into a chilly, cramped lobby painted an unfortunate shade of green. A door to her left stood open. She heard Pat Montesque's unmistakable tones in the room beyond.

"This was intended as a meeting of church officers, and although Jessica is of course welcome, she is not an elected officer. That was my only point."

The light in the hall was greenish too. Almost as if you were under water, Faith thought. The windows were set high off the floor so that in times past the school's Victorian pupils could not look out during lessons and be distracted by thoughts of the great world beyond. Columns of plastic chairs stood stacked either side of a plain oak cabinet which might have been a valuable antique had it been waxed up and placed in the right sale. The far end of the hall was dominated by a hessian hanging, appliquéd with a vast stylized dove of peace flying from an orange sun with gold thread rays. Set dead centre before it, Pat Montesque, Fred Partridge and the blonde woman server from the church sat grouped on the far side of a long wooden table, as if they were about to take part in a tableau of Da Vinci's *The Last Supper*.

"Reverend Morgan!" Fred Partridge pushed back his seat and came towards her, clearly grateful for the interruption. "So pleased you are able to join us. We are so grateful for you stepping in like this in the midst of all this…" He ran out of words. Faith silently sympathized. She wasn't sure of the proper phrase to describe the murder of one's vicar, either.

"I am glad to do anything I can to help, but please, call me Faith."

She heard Pat Montesque snort.

"Such a pretty name, and how appropriate to my mind," Fred said cheerily. "Now, I don't think you've been introduced."

He ushered Faith across to where the pretty blonde stood shyly beside Pat. "This is Jessica, Jessica Rose, one of our servers and very much involved in the parish. You will have seen her on…" Again his words petered out. Ordinary words were insufficient to the extraordinary circumstances that had brought them together.

Faith shook hands. Jessica's grip was firmer than she expected. Close up she could see her face was expertly made up to accentuate her striking blue eyes and long black lashes. She wore a sad, stunned look. Somehow she invited protection. Faith had an absurd desire to keep hold of her hand and comfort her.

"Jessica's a newcomer to the village," Pat Montesque's voice cut in. "Divorced. Arrived barely a year ago, but she was very close to the vicar."

Now that was nasty, thought Faith, and she gave the older

woman a firm look. Pat flinched, abashed. Faith immediately felt bad. Pat Montesque, it seemed, was one of those pushing women who frequently spoke before realizing how their words would sound out in the public domain.

"Jessica is an accountant. She does a lot of voluntary work for the diocese and its projects." Fred Partridge rushed to fill the gap. "She even gave up her holiday to go out to Africa last spring to work as a volunteer on one of the diocese's charitable projects." Jessica looked embarrassed.

"That must have been rather hot," Faith heard herself saying. "Fair-skinned, like me," she elaborated. "I find hot climates a bit of a trial."

"It was warm," Jessica responded, and managed a smile.

It was a getting-to-know-you meeting. Faith got out her diary and obediently made notes of Pat's instructions about where "the vicar" was expected to be and when. As the notations spread out across Palm Sunday and Holy Week, Faith felt a combination of thrill and awe. She was about to preside over her first Easter celebrations as vicar in charge.

"We're fortunate that Canon Arbuthnot from the cathedral has agreed to cover the Easter Day service," said Pat, ticking another item off her list. "At a time like this, I think the congregation would like the comfort of someone with authority."

Fred looked embarrassed. Faith lifted her eyebrows. She decided to let it pass and discuss that with the bishop later. Eventually Pat reached the end of her list. Faith closed her diary and put it in her bag.

"Perhaps a cup of tea?" said Fred.

"I'll make it." Jessica stood and left the room without waiting for a reply.

Pat watched her go. "She was friendly with Trevor Shoesmith, of course," she said.

Fred's frown looked incongruous on his round face. Faith knew she shouldn't be joining in gossip, but she couldn't help herself.

"The farmer?"

"The man the police took away this morning," responded Pat with heavy significance. "She spent quite a bit of time over there on Trevor Shoesmith's farm. Riding." She looked over the bridge of her small nose.

"From what I understand, Mr Shoesmith was just invited in for a chat. That's merely routine," Faith said briskly, cross with herself for encouraging Pat. "In a village like this, I suppose you all know each other." She looked to Fred for support. He was examining his chubby hands resting on the tabletop. "The police will be asking questions of everyone. It's what they do."

Pat didn't seem convinced. Fred was surprisingly silent. Jessica returned with the tea. She must have known they had been talking about her.

"We've been discussing Trevor Shoesmith," said Faith as she accepted her cup of tea. Pat started. "There's something I need to mention," Faith continued. "I know that neighbours talk to one another – and they should – but the bishop has asked me to warn you that it is likely the press may get on to this sad event." She chose her words carefully. "The bishop hopes that all the faithful members of this congregation and most especially their officers" – she glanced at Pat – "will do their best to dampen speculation."

The older woman bridled.

"Well! Of course! Naturally we don't want journalists poking their noses in around here. If I see any of those, I shall give them a piece of my mind!"

Faith's heart sank. "Perhaps it might be better just to avoid them." She passed out the Reverend Casey's cards. "The bishop suggests that any enquiries be referred to the diocesan press officer."

"I need to mention something," Fred said suddenly. "It's worrying me. I don't know that it should – but it is." He paused. "They're saying it's pesticide."

Faith frowned, trying to follow his meaning.

"I'm a farmer's merchant," Fred explained.

"But Trevor – Mr Shoesmith," Jessica corrected herself hurriedly, "doesn't use pesticide; he believes it poisons the land."

"Nonsense!" said Pat. "Mind you," the churchwarden wrinkled her button nose disapprovingly, "there's certainly no evidence that he does employ such aids or that land of his would look a good deal tidier."

"That's just it, I sold him some the other week," said Fred, his forehead creased in anxious lines. "Not much. Just a two-litre tin. He said he wanted to try an experiment." He fixed his round blue eyes on Faith. "Should I tell the police? That's what I want to know. It could look bad, and…"

"Of course you mustn't say!" All eyes swung to Jessica, startled by her vehemence. She faced them defiantly. "You can't go spreading tales like that. We don't know anything. The police haven't even confirmed pesticide. Gossip like that can ruin a man's reputation – and there's nothing behind it." She shifted back in her chair as if conscious that she had been too fervent.

"It's ridiculous to think poor Trevor could have anything to do with it. What could possibly be his motive?" Her eyes were pleading. "How can we think such things of our neighbour?"

The question lingered uncomfortably in the air and broke up their meeting. Jessica left first, murmuring something about an appointment, and Pat Montesque bustled out after her. Faith volunteered to wash up the tea things with Fred in the kitchen behind the hall.

"Fred," she shook the suds from the teacup and passed it to him to dry. "If you like, I could have a word with the sergeant about that sale and see what he thinks."

That would be best, she thought. Peter would be sensible about it.

The line of Fred's shoulders relaxed a fraction as if a weight had lifted from them.

"Could you really?" he asked eagerly. "I would be so grateful." He gave the cup an extra polish. "You know, we really are very lucky to have you."

Half an hour later, the motorway was unreeling in front of her in the blustery spring sunshine. The trip to Birmingham took two hours and twenty minutes when the traffic was loose. She liked driving. Time to think. Time to consider.

She had a collection of her favourite musicals stacked up in the CD player. It was a guilty pleasure. The great musical songs, she told herself, were like bright-as-paint fragments of the human condition – uplifting, direct. When the curtain came down you returned to real life somehow comforted. She switched the CD player onto random and settled in for the drive.

She shook her head, smiling wryly. On Saturday, she had been a curate investigating her options. Now it was Monday. She had witnessed a murder and been put in charge (temporary charge, she corrected herself) of a parish – the scene of the crime. And the scene of the crime was Ben's crime scene. Was this supposed to happen?

The CD track had switched to *Chicago*. She thought it ironic that the song currently playing was "He had it coming". She sang along under her breath.

It had taken such effort to switch paths; to change herself from policewoman to an ordained minister of the church. It had been a challenge she had felt she had had to take, but it hadn't been without cost. The discipline had been hard. She had cut herself off from her old life – even, in a way, from her old self. And now, it seemed fate, or God, had catapulted her into collision with Ben and the police and herself and her past choices; it all seemed to be rolled into one vast confusing imponderable open-ended... mess? Adventure? Challenge? Something!

Couldn't resist touching the body, eh? She heard Ben's voice, teasing, sarcastic.

The uncomfortable truth was that he was right. Alistair Ingram's death had reawakened a part of her she thought she'd left behind. She, Faith Morgan, liked investigating; talking to people, analyzing their expressions, reading their body language, peering into their lives; fitting together the broken puzzle of what they said and didn't say, and why. She was good at it.

In her mind's eye she saw Peter Gray, the first moment they'd met, flipping out his warrant card.

Be honest.

All right. The authority of the police role was attractive: a card-carrying purveyor of justice. There. She'd said it.

What was it you left behind? The question popped up and caught her by surprise.

What was that?

What had she been leaving behind? Ben? The police? And was it really a question of either/or?

She had the powerful feeling that God was leading her somewhere. She spoke to the humming silence inside her car – "Did you intend this?"

No answer.

"Was I supposed to join your team? Did I misread the signals?" she asked.

The player seemed to have paused. Then another CD fell into place in the changer. *Oliver.* Nancy's rousing anthem soared – the song was "As long as he needs me".

She laughed out loud.

CHAPTER
6

THE BEATLES' GREATEST HITS WERE PLAYING as she opened the door. Her mother liked her to have a key so she could let herself in. Her great-grandmother's blue china dog grinned at her from the hall table. That dog had sat on the hall table in every house her mother had lived in from as far back as Faith could remember. Just the sight of it made her feel as if she were home.

"Mum!"

"In here!" trilled her mother's voice from the front room above the strains of *Sgt Pepper's Lonely Hearts Club Band*.

Faith rounded the corner to see her mother perched precariously in her stockinged feet on the back of the sofa, hanging a curtain. Marianne Morgan was petite like her eldest daughter, Ruth, and she had to stretch. There were two spots of colour on her cheekbones and she was puffing with the effort of it.

"Mum! You shouldn't be doing that!"

Marianne forced the last hook into position. "There!"

She wobbled as she bent to get down. Faith barely reached her in time.

"Oof! Not getting any younger," Marianne said cheerfully, slipping her shoes back on. She still wore heels. Even though she'd turned seventy, she had good ankles.

"Hello, dear. You made good time. Mr Clean just dropped these off and I wanted to get them up before supper."

"Mr Clean" ran the dry-cleaning business around the corner. Marianne had always made friends easily and Mr Clean, being from Pakistan and respectful of elderly ladies, treated her with special kindness.

"That was very kind of him, but if you weren't going to wait for me you should still have used a stepladder," Faith said, giving her a hug.

"Of course, dear," her mother replied with a complete lack of sincerity. "Let's have a sherry. I've just come off the phone to Ruth. What on earth has been happening down in Little Worthy?"

Her mother poured them both a glass of her favourite pale cream sherry. Faith had never liked it as a drink, but it was a ritual they shared. Her mother always drank her sherry from the remnants of a set of waisted glasses Dad had picked up years ago – a special offer from the Esso station with every purchase over five pounds. Dad had loved his bargains.

"So the vicar of Little Worthy, poisoned before your very eyes with the communion wine?" Mum had never been mealy-mouthed.

"Sounds like Ruth's filled you in."

"Well, I have to say that village was always a bit sly for my tastes," Marianne took a sip of sherry and rolled it around her mouth before swallowing. "Everybody was always trying to keep up a façade of some sort."

Façade. Don had said the same thing.

"I didn't realize you knew Little Worthy?"

"Oh yes. The head of the Mother's Union used to hold court there at one point while we lived in Winchester. I suppose you would have been at primary school at the time. Dreadful woman!"

"Really?" asked Faith, intrigued. As her mother grew older, she became increasingly decisive in her opinions.

"She's long gone." Marianne dismissed the subject. "And Ben Shorter's in charge of the investigation? That's a surprise for you." Her mother cocked her head at her.

Faith shrugged. "I knew he was back in Winchester in the CID. He's already collected a suspect: the farmer who lives next door to the vicarage – a Trevor Shoesmith."

"Trevor Shoesmith?" Marianne sat bolt upright in her chair. "Not Fran and Bill Shoesmith's boy? That can't be right."

"You knew them?" asked Faith. Why was she surprised? she thought. Her mother knew everyone.

"The Shoesmiths? Oh yes. They've been dead for years. Such tragedy that family suffered; and as for Trevor, what a sad boy he was – gentle as anything. He wouldn't hurt a fly."

"A tragedy? What was that?"

"Now let me think," Marianne looked into the middle distance, her glass of sherry balanced, forgotten, on the arm of her chair. "It must have been well over twenty years ago. There was an accident on the farm and the eldest boy was killed. It was doubly awful because Trevor was involved in some way. He was only fifteen."

"You mean he killed his brother?"

"Accidentally. There was no question about that. His father shouldn't have had those boys handling heavy machinery unsupervised; the other boy was barely a year older. Bill was as much to blame as anyone. The family was devastated."

"When did the parents die?"

"They went – oh! – fifteen years later, or more. Died within a few weeks of one another. They were a devoted couple." Faith recognized the note in her mother's voice; Marianne disapproved in some way. "He went with cancer, I think, then Fran followed with a heart attack not long after. Poor Trevor."

"Why so?"

"I said they were devoted. Too much so, maybe. I think the poor boy rather lost out," Marianne said crisply. Faith smiled at her. Her mother had always been warmly concerned for her own children. "As I say, he was such a sad boy. A bit of a born loser."

A sad boy; a born loser. The thought of another sad boy just like that jumped into Faith's mind. Richard Fisher. The case that had first come between her and Ben; the first time she had seen the worst side of him – implacable, driven and unforgiving. She had a moment of dread. What if that should happen again with Trevor Shoesmith, all because she had pointed him out to Ben?

"You're quiet," her mother said. "There's been rather a lot going on, hasn't there?" She was still, her face concerned.

"I'm fine, Mum. Really." Faith took a deep breath. "There's rather a lot to think about, that's all. You know the bishop has asked me to cover St James's for the interim?"

"That's a step up."

"It's only temporary." Faith was embarrassed. Her mother's turn of phrase made it sound as if she were profiteering by death. "The bishop only asked me to help as I was on the spot."

"Nonsense," said her mother. "He'd already invited you to look round *and* he invited you to lunch." In Marianne's world, social niceties meant something. "How did that go, by the way?"

Faith smiled, relieved to be able to talk about something else. "The Beeches are good people. Very into their missionary work. They were out in Tanzania for years." She thought of the faces of Alison and Anthony as they'd talked about Africa. "I think they left a bit of their hearts there. Mrs Beech insisted on going personally to the hospital to check on the victim's son, Don. He's a friend of Sean's, you know."

"Don Ingram? Of course. I know Don," Marianne made a sympathetic clucking noise with her tongue against her teeth. "One of Sean's set at school. Rather good-looking. They're up at university together. How's he doing?"

"Not sure." Faith thought of Don's odd manner. "I'm trying to keep an eye on him. He's very much on his own now."

"Of course, his mother died – of cancer; another one. At least he has Sean."

Faith was surprised by her mother's assurance. "Mum – how do you know all this? I didn't even recognize him when I met him."

"Well, you should pay more attention," said her mother. "You'll be moving in with your sister for the duration, I suppose?"

Ruth had been very generous. She had assured Faith she could have the spare room for as long as she liked. Faith took a deep breath. The thought of her elder sister scrutinizing her every move and prodding her about Ben as she tried to negotiate the rapids ahead made her heart sink. Still, family were important.

Her mother was looking right into her.

Faith got up and sat on the floor beside her mother's chair and put her head in her lap as she used to do when she was little. Her mother's hand stroked her hair.

"So what's the problem, sweetheart?"

Faith breathed in her mother's comforting scent of wool and soap and Yardley's cologne.

"I don't know that I'm up to this, Mum. I'm trying. But I'm just not sure what I'm supposed to do – what the right thing is."

Her mother placed a kiss on the top of her head.

"Maybe it's not a matter of guessing what the right way is," she said. "Maybe God wants you to be yourself and live life in your own way. We are supposed to be made in His image, after all." She turned her daughter to face her. "Aren't we?"

"That's a profound thought, Mother."

"Thank you, dear. I blame the sherry. Shall we eat?"

After supper, they said their goodbyes and Faith returned to her flat. It was a modern conversion on the first floor of an Edwardian terraced house near her parish church. She had a living room with the kitchen at one end, one bedroom and a bathroom. She liked the high ceilings, and the living room had an attractive bay window. She had left in daylight and the curtains were drawn back. When she closed the door behind her, she didn't turn on the light at first. She stood in the orange glow of the street lamp, looking around.

What was she supposed to pack? She didn't know how long she would be in Little Worthy. She thought of Ruth's cramped spare room with the Cabbage Patch dolls. She felt a pang at the thought of separation from the things that made her space her own. A pair of nineteenth-century seascapes she'd found in a junk shop in Southampton; the battered trophy she had won in a dinghy sailing competition in the Solent, aged twelve; the illustrated edition of *Sherlock Holmes* her father had given her when she passed out of Hendon. They were like whorls and loops on the fingerprint of her life.

The stillness in the flat was palpable. She picked up the phone and dialled.

"Meg, I am sorry to call so late, but is Jonathan around? I was hoping to speak to him."

"Faith! Of course," said Meg. "We've been thinking about you. Here he is."

Meg passed the phone over to her husband, and Canon Jonathan's voice came on.

"Faith, you've been having terrifying times, I hear," he said in his usual dry way. She felt her eyes tear up.

"So-so," she said.

"Alistair Ingram. He died in the middle of the service?"

"Yes."

She heard the intake of his breath.

"I knew him – well, I'd met him. Alistair was often called in to address diocesan seminars. He was very good on finances; a wizard at fund-raising. Had some impressive contacts in the city."

"He was poisoned. Pesticide in the communion wine."

"Dear God! Anyone else hurt?"

She was finding it oddly difficult to speak. "No. It happened quickly. He drank and that was it."

"How are you holding up?" he asked. "How do you feel about being parachuted in to look after the parish?"

"I'm not entirely sure what I am doing," she said. Her voice quavered. She paused to pull herself together. She looked around at her flat. "I don't know what to pack," she heard herself say, and gave a small, shaky laugh.

"Right," he said briskly. Jonathan always understood. "Unfortunately I have to go out now."

"Bible class," Faith said. Bible class was always held on a Monday night.

"How about you come and see me tomorrow morning. We can have a chat?"

"I'd love to, but I've got to pack. It's over two hours' drive back, and I'm expected in Little Worthy."

"You come and say Matins with me – 7 a.m.," Jonathan said in his rector's voice. Faith heard Meg's voice indistinct in the background.

"Meg says she can come over and help you pack after that. She's offering breakfast." The warmth of their kindness steadied her.

"Thank you. By the way, the Little Worthy investigation, it is still ongoing. I'm not sure the details are supposed to be public knowledge."

"Don't worry. We shan't be repeating anything."

"Thanks."

"See you tomorrow, then. You go have a bath and get some sleep."

She did just that. But after her bath, she checked her emails and felt a fresh flush of annoyance at the stuffy form of words George Casey had sent her. That man! She hovered the mouse over delete, but thought better of it. Instead, she switched off the computer and took out her *Book of Common Prayer*. She liked the idea of it – that all across the church over the hours of that evening, thousands upon thousands would repeat the same words; pray the same prayers. She read the Collect of the day to herself – taking care with the words. She was reading the psalm when a couplet sprang out at her.

Stand in awe, and sin not:
Commune with your own heart upon your bed, and be still.

She went to bed comforted. Good fellowship and good people, she thought, as she drifted off, and in her imagination she felt God smile.

CHAPTER

7

FAITH PARKED HER CAR ON THE GREEN across from
the church. Down the lane she could see the corner of Trevor
Shoesmith's farmhouse through the trees. It was barely 11:10 a.m.
She'd made Little Worthy in record time.

She wound down her window. There was a chill in the air
today. Stratocumulus clouds, low and clumpy, were gathering
across the sky. The green was as pretty as a print; a smooth, pastoral
expanse bordered with white and timber-framed cottages, some
with low-pitched roofs of dense thatch, standing back behind
colourful gardens. It was a people-less idyll. Everyone seemed to
be at work. It took money to own a house on the green.

She was in uniform today – a soft ivory clerical shirt and dog
collar matched with a russet tweed skirt and boots in concession
to the cooler weather. She felt the breeze on her skin. She was
faintly embarrassed about her weak moment of the day before.
She'd set the alarm for 5:30, but woken full of energy when it was
still dark at ten past. She mused for a moment on the mysteries
of the internal body clock. Whenever she set her alarm on an
important day she always seemed to wake up by herself twenty
minutes before it was due to go off.

Matins with Canon Jonathan had felt like a farewell. It was
odd. For all its familiarity, the echoing Victorian church of St
Michael's had seemed distanced, as if she had already peeled herself

off from her previous life. Perhaps the pain and confusion she'd experienced last night had been the moment of severance. She had woken with a clearer head, her mind focused on the challenge ahead. Jonathan and Meg had waved her off on the road soon after eight. Filled with friendship and Meg's home-made muesli, she drove away from the parish that had been her home for more than two years without a backward glance.

She caught sight of her suitcase in the mirror. It loomed behind her on the back seat. Ruth wouldn't get home from work until five. Faith had no fixed appointments until her meeting with the rural dean at four. She felt untethered. Fred had given her a set of keys to St James's at their meeting yesterday afternoon. Perhaps she should go in and familiarize herself with her new church.

The image of Alistair Ingram's crumpled body behind the altar sprang up, and she shied away from the idea.

Dear Lord, help me with this day!

St James's looked down on her from its rising ground. From her vantage point there was no hint of the horror that had taken place just two days ago. The grass in the graveyard was trim and the shrubs along the path well cared for. She was responsible for this place of worship – even if only temporarily. She felt the awe of such a duty of care.

This church has endured here for over 900 years; it looks so neat and tidy now, she told herself, but just think of what this building has weathered through time – marauders, civil war, epidemics, famine – and now murder. It is still standing. It represents love and redemption.

Sin shall not have dominion over you.

You shouldn't be afraid.

She spoke the Lord's Prayer aloud in her car.

"… thine is the kingdom, and the power, and the glory, for ever and ever. Amen."

She knew what she needed to do. She would organize an event to reclaim St James's from the awful desecration of the weekend. On Thursday perhaps. In her mind's eye, she saw members of the congregation cleaning the church and saying prayers for Alistair Ingram. They needed to face what had happened as a community, and reassert the true purpose of the building as a house of God and love.

She would speak to the rural dean about it that afternoon.

But first she should check on the living – she would see if Don was in. She bent down to gather up her handbag.

As she straightened up, she caught a flash of colour behind the trees out of the corner of her eye. Someone was taking a short cut from the direction of Trevor Shoesmith's farmhouse. It was a woman. Faith caught a glimpse of blonde hair. She recognized Jessica Rose.

Jessica was carrying a bright beach bag over one shoulder. Faith watched idly. The bag's gaudy flamboyance seemed incongruous. Jessica had struck her as a woman who dressed to blend in, not stand out.

Jessica approached the church, half screened by the trees. As she passed a gap, Faith thought she saw the imprint of something boxy stretching the fabric of the bag.

Jessica walked up to the church, unlocked the vestry door, and went in.

That's odd, Faith thought. Pat Montesque's complaint, overheard before the meeting in the church hall, echoed in her memory: *although Jessica is of course welcome, she is not an elected officer.*

Why should Jessica have a key to the church?

Maybe it's because she does the flowers; you're being ridiculous! Faith told herself. Stop seeing conspiracy everywhere. There is probably a perfectly innocent explanation.

Should she go in too, and have a word?

She stayed in the car.

A dove, as white as snow, flew down and perched on the yew tree by the church gate. It preened itself and cooed. There must be a dovecote nearby.

Barely a minute or so passed and Jessica came out of the

vestry again. She locked the door, glancing around hurriedly – almost furtively, thought Faith; will she see me watching?

But Jessica just hurried off with her head down, clutching the flat beach bag to her chest, returning the way she'd come.

She watched Jessica's fleeting form through the trees until it dropped out of sight in the lane.

Faith sat considering what she'd seen. Through the open window she heard an engine start up. In her wing mirror she saw a silver car come out of the lane leading to Shoesmith's farm. As it paused to turn onto the green, she caught a glimpse of Jessica at the wheel. The car sped off in the direction of Alresford and disappeared.

Faith rummaged in her bag. Finally her fingers found the elusive piece of card. She took out her mobile and dialled.

There were roadworks on the way into Winchester and the traffic was bad. Faith had trouble finding a parking place. She was ten minutes later than she'd intended when she entered the café round the corner from the police station. Peter was sitting at a table by the picture window with two coffees in front of him, his eyes fixed on the screen of his mobile. He looked up as she walked in, and rose to his feet to greet her.

"Thanks for meeting me at such short notice," Faith said, putting out her hand. Her fingers were cushioned momentarily in his large palm.

"No trouble," Peter said. "I ordered you coffee – hope that's OK?" He looked at it dubiously. "It's better than the tea – usually."

"That's fine." She sat down opposite him. His jacket was open. She noticed that his buttons strained a little against the fabric of his shirt, as if he'd recently put on weight. He smoothed down his tie.

"So, what's up?" he said.

Faith took a deep breath. "I have some information – it may mean nothing…"

Peter cocked his head. *He's wondering why I'm not talking to Ben*, she thought.

I'm not talking to Ben because he'll probably take it the wrong way.

No. She couldn't say that. Better just to plough on.

"I have been talking to the churchwardens at St James's. Fred Partridge – the man with me when we first met? He's a farmer's merchant."

"Has a business on the road to Alresford. I know," Peter nodded encouragingly.

"Well, everyone agrees that Trevor Shoesmith doesn't use pesticide. He has always been insistent about not believing in spreading chemicals about, apparently – but Fred mentioned that he'd sold him some just the other week."

Peter leaned forward.

"Not much," Faith continued – *which makes it all the more suspicious*, her inner voice added in silent commentary in her head. "But Fred was surprised at the time, and now he's concerned. It's not that he thinks Trevor's done anything, but…" she trailed off.

Peter raised his eyebrows.

"I know," she responded, "but I've been talking to my mother." Now, that sounded silly. She began again. "My mother used to live round here." Faith struggled to find the words to justify her trust in her mother's judgment. "She knew the Shoesmiths – both the parents and Trevor too."

Peter looked polite.

Now she said it aloud, how flimsy it sounded! *This man I've never met just couldn't be a murderer because my mother says so.* It was a good thing she'd chosen to speak to Peter rather than Ben; at least he had the good manners to hear her out as if he were actually interested.

"She told me about a family tragedy – in Shoesmith's past, and…"

"When he was fifteen he killed his elder brother in a farming accident," Peter supplied calmly, and drank some coffee.

"You know about it?"

He swallowed. "There's a file." He put down his cup. "Turned it up on the background check. He had some counselling afterwards. There's a report from some psychiatrist that says he was depressive."

"Well, he might be! My mother described him as a sad boy and a loser."

"But she knew him in his teens…?"

"And twenties," cut in Faith. She knew what was coming.

"OK. But even given that, he's what – in his early forties now? A lot can change a man in that time."

"But time doesn't change fundamental character," she insisted. "Trevor Shoesmith sounds like someone who's self-destructive, if anything. Look at the farm. That's not the farm of a man who takes action."

Peter shrugged. "Maybe. But that's speculation. You know the inspector: *ABC – Assume nothing…*'

"*Believe nothing. Check everything!*" Faith chimed in.

"So he's always been like this?" Peter grinned.

"Oh yes!" Faith smiled back wryly. She looked down at the dregs in her cup. He was right, of course. She knew what Ben was like; that's why she was talking to Peter. And what on earth was she expecting him to do?

"There's something else, isn't there?" Peter asked.

She lifted her eyes to meet his; they were sympathetic.

"The reason I called you…" Here I go again, she thought. "I was parked outside the church and I saw Jessica Rose coming from the direction of Trevor Shoesmith's farm with this big bag – a beach bag. Completely out of season!" She tried to make a joke of it. "Anyway, I'd swear there was something bulky in it. She went into the church, and then she came out minutes later and whatever was in the bag was gone."

"You're sure?"

Faith bit her lip and grimaced. "I'm sure."

"She didn't see you?"

"No. The church is on rising ground and there's the wall. I was parked on the other side of it. I could see her, but I think all she'd see was the top of the car, not me in it."

She looked at Peter across the table. His face was solemn.

"You're observant," he commented.

If Ben had said those words they would have been loaded with sarcasm. Peter clearly meant it as a compliment. Faith felt embarrassed.

"Some might call it nosey." Might as well make a complete report. She told him about Jessica driving off in her silver car. That old Hendon training was hard to shake.

Peter was looking into the middle distance. "How come she had keys to the church?" he asked. He turned back to her. "It was locked, I presume?"

It was Faith's turn to be impressed. Peter was quick.

"I know, I wondered about that," she agreed. "She's not a churchwarden. Maybe she had a key so she could do the flowers or something."

"I thought you didn't have flowers in the church over Lent."

"It varies from church to church."

"Oh."

Their eyes met over the tabletop, their expressions solemn.

"I'm going to have to tell the boss."

"Of course." She'd always known that Ben would have to know. She just hadn't wanted to face him herself. The truth, she told herself sternly, was that she wanted to participate without taking responsibility for the consequences. Ben was right; she was a coward.

Peter made up his mind about something. "Jessica Rose's name has already come up in the investigation," he said.

"Really?" She could sense his excitement. He was bubbling over with the desire to share some discovery with her.

"When we went to interview Shoesmith at the farm – to ask him about his dispute with the vicar – the boss spotted this letter.

It was in plain sight; on the desk. And you know the boss – he's got eagle eyes. Never leave anything around you don't want him to see." Peter's admiration for Ben saturated his voice.

Ben had that effect on his juniors, reflected Faith. They hero-worshipped him. Especially the young men; the women just fell for him.

"What was the letter?" she prompted, just to be saying something.

Peter leaned forward. He looked like an eager small boy in a grown-up's suit.

"A love letter from Trevor to Jessica." He sat back trying to look like a man of the world, but the tips of his ears were blushing with his enthusiasm. "He had a thing for her."

Faith thought of the woman she had met so briefly; was she the type to be having a clandestine relationship with an inadequate farmer? She could imagine men of all kinds would be drawn to Jessica's blue-eyed prettiness. She had an element of Marilyn Monroe's sexy vulnerability about her. But as another woman, her impression of Jessica had been of someone tender-hearted and self-effacing. She thought of Jessica rocking beside the fallen vicar, and then her vehemence when they'd discussed reporting Fred's sale in the church hall – had that been more than a sensitive person's Christian concern for a neighbour?

"Was it a two-way relationship?" she voiced the question out loud. "Were there others – other letters?"

"Not in plain sight." Peter shrugged. "We didn't have a warrant."

Searching without a warrant would make any evidence inadmissible in court. Ben was a stickler for details like that. He prided himself on delivering a sound chain of evidence to the prosecution service.

"The letter wasn't finished," Peter explained. "That's why it was out on the desk."

"What did Trevor say about it?"

"He wouldn't say much about anything – very quiet."

Faith had a vision of a silent, sad man living alone in the midst of that rundown farm. The more she heard, the more she saw Trevor Shoesmith as a vulnerable victim, not a murderer.

"So – do you think Jessica Rose is helping him?" Peter prompted, leaning across the table towards her. "Shoesmith's a self-declared atheist. He was never known to set foot in the church. It would make more sense if he had inside help to get the poison in the wine."

"Oh no!" Faith thought of Jessica with her sad blue eyes and gentle manner. She knew it was only in films that people like that turned out to be psychos. In real life, very few people had the talent for that level of deception.

"I just don't buy any of it!" she exclaimed with more fervour than she'd intended. "Trevor as the poisoner, or Jessica helping him. Just think about it! If Trevor the atheist wants to murder the vicar, why on earth would he choose to use communion wine? How many murders – planned murders – have you heard of where the first-time killer chooses to do the deed somewhere unfamiliar? The church is alien territory to Trevor Shoesmith."

The more she talked the more passionate she felt, and the more sure she was that she was right.

"Whoever put the poison in the wine knew about the ritual and habits of that church – when the wine was decanted, who would drink it first – and how to get hold of the keys to get in. Trevor lives next to the vicarage. He can watch the vicar go in and out. If he's going to use poison, isn't he going to plant something in the man's kitchen? Leave him some nice fresh poisoned mushrooms on his doorstep or something?"

Peter put his hands up. "All right! All right! You have your doubts about Shoesmith as a suspect."

"Sorry!" Faith apologized, rueful at her outburst. "But you see what I mean?"

Peter nodded. "I do." He almost looked convinced. "But the boss is in charge of the case. It's up to him. He'll figure it out," he said, with absolute confidence.

She felt a twinge of regret. Once she'd felt the same confidence in Ben. Then she'd lost her innocence.

The face of Richard Fisher squatted in the back of her mind. The features were blurred after all these years, but she could still feel the drag of his desperate nothingness.

She gave herself a mental shake. She was being unfair to Ben. Richard Fisher belonged to another time, another place. These were different circumstances. They were two very different cases. Ben could ride roughshod, but he was a good investigator – and he believed in justice; she knew he did. In the end, Ben would build his case on facts.

Peter was watching her with a perplexed look.

"Where is he now – Trevor Shoesmith?" she asked.

"Back at his place. We don't have the evidence to charge him. The boss is working on getting a warrant to search the house. He's got the RSPCA coming in later today to take away the animals."

"That bad?"

She thought of the pony in the weeds. She wasn't a horse person but Jessica, apparently, was. According to Pat Montesque, Jessica often went riding at Trevor's place. That was another piece that didn't fit. Could gentle Jessica be a fake? Was she likely to overlook cruelty, or be attracted to someone who was deliberately unkind to animals?

Peter's face was serious as he contemplated the state of Trevor Shoesmith's animals.

"Pretty bad."

"I wonder if Trevor Shoesmith's having a breakdown," said Faith. "Aren't you worried about him?"

"We can't move any faster."

Faith had an overwhelming sense of dread and sadness. This tragedy hadn't run its course yet. She pushed the thought away.

"I should get going." She picked up her bag. "You'll need to be getting back to the station, and I should look in on Don Ingram."

Peter wasn't paying attention. He looked startled. She followed his gaze over her shoulder.

Ben was standing in the doorway of the café, glaring at them.

CHAPTER
8

BEN ATE UP THE DISTANCE BETWEEN THEM in long strides. Peter sprang to his feet. Ben was one table away when his phone rang. He stopped dead, a look of annoyance on his face. He flipped his mobile open.

"Shorter!" His expression changed. Faith knew that look. A lady friend. Ben's head dropped and he turned away as he listened. The line of his back was expressive. Faith heard herself snort. It was very faint. No one else could have heard it.

The lady friend was probably whispering sweet nothings in his ear. Faith imagined a twenty-something with improbably long legs. Perhaps she was perky, or maybe reproachful.

Ben grunted monosyllabically. Faith recognized the code. There had been a time when she was the woman on the other end of that call. Then she'd been the one wondering why the man who had felt so close hours previously had assumed such distance. She'd never really learned to live with it.

Ben murmured something. He snapped the phone shut. He turned back towards them, his posture rigid and his eyes flat.

"Is this a private meeting, or can anyone join in?"

Faith was annoyed. He might be cross with her, but it was unprofessional to show it in front of his staff. Peter was looking distinctly uncomfortable. Faith's chin rose.

"The sergeant gave me his number," she said. "I assumed you

would be busy."

"As is my sergeant," Ben retorted brusquely.

Peter looked between them. He cleared his throat.

"Faith – Ms Morgan…" Ben flicked him a cynical look. "She has information pertinent to the case."

"Oh yes?"

"She saw Mrs Jessica Rose sneaking into the church," said Peter in a rush.

Faith grimaced internally at Peter's choice of words. Surely she hadn't described Jessica as *sneaking* – had she?

"It seems Mrs Rose had come from Shoesmith's farm," Peter was saying, "and it looks like she may have dumped something at the church."

"Been twitching the net curtains?" Ben said, looking down on her from his great height. "You've taken to village life!"

Faith just managed to stop herself reacting. He'd always had the unerring ability to prod where it hurt. She'd come to St James's to serve the congregation, not to inform on them. She wanted to stand up, but she wouldn't give Ben the satisfaction. She deliberately relaxed her tense shoulders, feeling the wooden support of the chair at her back. She gazed at him with what she hoped resembled pleasant detachment.

And you wonder why I chose to talk to Peter, she thought.

For a moment, she imagined he'd heard her. The corner of Ben's mouth twitched. He looked at his sergeant and jerked his head.

"Brief me," he said, and took Peter aside.

She watched as Peter updated his boss in a low voice. She didn't catch most of it. Ben heard him out without interruption. Throughout he kept his eyes on Faith, as if he were weighing her up from a distance. She began to feel quite hot. Anger built up inside her. She was not going to sit here and take this.

Just as she was making up her mind to leave, Ben walked back.

"You've got keys?"

She looked at him blankly.

"To the church?" he elaborated impatiently.

Silently she nodded.

"Come on, then!"

"What are you talking about?" Faith exclaimed. He had no right to order her about.

He quirked an eyebrow. "If you give information to the investigating team, I investigate."

She felt such a fool. He was quite right. What did she expect?

"I'd like to get to it before someone comes along and fouls things up," he prompted.

"It's not convenient; I have other things to do." She meant to be dignified but it came out as stubborn. Ben waited. Without saying a word, he conveyed his doubt that she did have anything better to do. Faith bit her lip.

"Oh, for God's sake!" She grabbed her bag and followed him to the door.

There, he'd made her blaspheme in front of the sergeant. Ben looked smug. She glared him down. "Don't say it!" she hissed.

Ben held the door open for her.

"I assumed you'd want to come," he said. His voice was like chocolate. "Shall I drive?"

She brushed past him.

"I'll meet you there," she snapped, and felt mildly better.

She was unfamiliar with the lock. It took her two tries to select the right key for the vestry door from the bunch that Fred Partridge had given her. All the while Faith was acutely conscious of Ben's presence at her shoulder. He had despatched Peter off on some other business. Alone together at last! She tried to appreciate the irony.

The lock protested and turned. Ben followed her into the musty chill of the vestry. He stood in the patch of light from the open door, pulling on a pair of latex gloves and looking around critically.

"What sort of size do you think this object was?"

"I can't be sure, but something like this?" Faith measured a space between her hands around the size of a four-pint carton of milk.

"You said she was only in here for a minute or so. It's likely to be somewhere fairly obvious."

He opened a cupboard door. The shelves were stacked with music sheets. He swung the door shut with a smart click and moved onto the next. Faith stood in the middle of the tiled floor. She wasn't sure what to do. She wondered if anyone had seen them come in.

She was embarrassed by the idea that she, the newcomer, the interloper, might be discovered by the churchwardens helping the police – in the person of her handsome ex (God help her if they knew that!) – pry into the nooks and crannies of their church. Put that way, it sounded distinctly objectionable.

Ben was crouched in front of the waist-high cupboard where celebrants would lay out their robes. He looked at her over his shoulder.

"Not going to help?"

"Like you said: you're the one who investigates."

He grunted and went on with his search.

He hauled out a case of wine. Bottles of communion wine. He examined them for a moment without touching. They were unopened, their seals intact. He ran a hand round the back of the cupboard and returned the case. His hands were black. He kicked the door shut as he moved on.

"Do try to remember that this is a place of worship," Faith scolded.

"You know it has to be done," he responded, irritatingly calm.

He ran his hands along the shelf above the rail of choir robes and came up with a slingshot, two marbles and a bunch of comics. One was yellowing and brittle. He read the masthead.

"This one's 1977. Don't believe in cleaning things out, do

they? But then the Church is all about tradition."

She narrowed her eyes at his back.

He threw her an indulgent glance over his shoulder. "You know, this will go much faster if you help." A grin flashed on his face, infectious, charming. "And if we find what we're looking for, maybe you won't get caught sneaking around like this."

Silently, he held out another pair of latex gloves.

Faith snatched them from him and pulled them on. She opened the vestment wardrobe behind her and joined in the search.

A few minutes later, they had been through every available hiding place in the vestry. They stood just inside the nave, each within their own space.

St James's, Little Worthy wasn't as large as some churches, but it was quite large enough. Faith's eyes scanned the pillars and pews with a sinking heart. This could take hours.

"You've lost your instincts." Ben's voice was smug.

"What?"

He strolled over to an old upright piano pushed back in the shadow of one wall.

"The first place an old-fashioned burglar would look – if he were the type on the lookout for church silver," he said. He opened the lid.

"Don't be silly," she scoffed. "They probably use that for choir practice. Put something in there and it'll foul the strings; make a clunking sound. Someone's bound to investigate."

He took a slim torch out of an inner pocket.

"Want to bet?" he said, shining the torch inside the case. He turned towards her and beckoned her over with one latex-gloved hand. She crossed over to him and looked in. There, lit up in the torch beam, was a brown paper bag wrapped around something about the right size.

"It would seem Mrs Rose isn't musical," he said.

Oh Jessica! She thought. What have you got yourself into?

Ben was dialling his phone.

"What are you going to do?"

"Get SOCO in. This should give us enough to move on Shoesmith." He read the look on her face and put his head down bullishly.

She stared down into the shadowy bowels of the case at the lighter patch that was the paper bag. She couldn't deny the obvious circumstantial evidence, but the people just didn't seem to fit the scenario. She was sure that something was badly wrong.

Ben finished his call.

"We have to wait until they get here. Damn! Should have kept the sergeant with me," he muttered.

She could feel his impatience to be off. He was as restless as a thoroughbred in the starting gate, bristling with energy.

"What?" he challenged her.

"You're so sure Trevor Shoesmith fits the bill?" Faith asked.

"You're not?" He stilled, searching her face. "You think I'm making it fit," he said slowly.

She didn't know what to say.

His expression froze. It was as if a trap door had opened up beneath their feet and they were back somewhere raw and intimate.

"His name's not Fisher," he said in a low voice.

She felt pierced by his eyes. There was anger behind them, and frustration and pain. Her throat closed. Her insides felt as if they were pushing to climb out of her mouth.

"I know."

"But you thought it."

It was true. She had thought of Richard Fisher. She tried to hold still but she couldn't help glancing down.

"No." She faced him squarely, her voice firm. "That was an entirely different case; a different time."

"Yes," he said. "It was." And he turned his back on her.

One pace away, he changed his mind and spun back.

"You're never going to forgive me for that, are you?" he demanded.

"It's not about forgiving you," Faith protested. "It's more about…" She swallowed the word she was about to use and substituted another. "… concern."

"Tcht!" Ben made an angry, dismissive noise.

Faith took a step towards him. "You don't pay enough account to humanity – the faces in the midst of all this; the individual persons."

Now she'd made him angry. He seemed to expand with energy and frustration.

"You know this job! I can't get all touchy-feely about the…" – he made savage air quotes around the word – "…*persons*. Do that and you lose your judgment. You make mistakes."

"Or you make mistakes because you don't."

She had a sudden comic vision of them facing off like cats in the house of God. Then it didn't feel so funny.

"But we're not talking in general. This is about Trevor Shoesmith," she said.

Ben shot her a cynical look.

"It doesn't seem to me that he fits with this…" – she waved a hand at the brown paper bag and its contents – "… this circumstantial evidence."

Ben snorted derisively. "You've never even laid eyes on the man!"

"But I've seen his farm; I've talked to people who know him. Everything points to a vulnerable man; a victim, not a murderer."

"Victims can pass it on."

She had to give him that. Violence and abuse often did breed the same. But then, although Trevor had suffered the trauma of his brother's death, there had been no murmur of anything else. According to her mother, the Shoesmiths had been an ordinary family that had suffered an extraordinary tragedy.

Ben was watching her think. His expression was warmer somehow. He cocked an eyebrow in silent query.

She acknowledged it ruefully.

"My first sight of Trevor Shoesmith's land was of a pony standing in a field of weeds." She had his full attention. No one could listen like Ben, when he chose to focus.

"Oh, I don't know!" She spread her hands, appealing for his comprehension. "It was so sad and lonely and pathetic."

"And that's how you see its owner?"

"Something like that. From what I hear, Trevor Shoesmith is entirely alone. If he isn't your man, just think what you…" she corrected herself hurriedly, "… the investigation must be putting him through."

He was silent for a moment. Then he shrugged.

"Can't afford to think about it. I have to follow the evidence."

The moment had passed. It was as if he had shrugged his armour back into place. They didn't speak another word. By the time the scene of crime team arrived five minutes later, they were standing a minimum of ten yards apart.

A crime scene photographer in overalls took pictures of the parcel in the piano case. Then they lifted it out and set it carefully on a pew for more photographs. Finally, Ben opened up the bag carefully and peered in. He looked up at Faith with the faun-ish expression she remembered so well.

"Bingo!"

Faith looked inside. It was a two-litre tin of pesticide. There were dark treacle-like stains around the cap.

The scene of crime officer was brushing powder over the piano lid with neat, economical strokes, his face intent. Faith stood by, watching him. She didn't want to stay, but she wasn't sure if she should leave the church unattended. Ben finished yet another phone call. He spoke in her direction, barely looking at her.

"I'll need your formal witness statement." He started walking to the door.

He was dismissing her. Faith felt the old stubbornness well

up inside her. No matter if she had no official right to be part of this investigation; she had a responsibility to the people of Little Worthy. She wasn't going to allow her personal witness to be reduced to the insufficient bare words of an official statement. She caught Ben up. She had to put a hand on his arm to stop him.

"Where are you going?"

He frowned and looked deliberately down at her hand, pale against the dark wool of his suit.

"The warrant's come through. I am going over to the farm."

"I'm coming with you," she said.

She had to see Trevor Shoesmith for herself – this time she would take responsibility for her actions.

"Suit yourself," Ben said, and he strode out ahead of her into the daylight.

CHAPTER
9

GREY CLOUDS HAD COVERED THE SKY. Rain was on its way. Faith could feel the first few specks in the breeze. Ben had long legs, and Faith struggled to keep up. She had only recently taken up jogging again. She congratulated herself on her foresight.

As they crossed the lane, she noticed a dash of colour on the pristine picture of the green. An old, dull red Ford Escort was parked on the far side. The driver was still sitting in it. A man; at this distance, a vague presence. He didn't get out. The first journalist, she thought. There would be more soon.

They were approaching the brick farmhouse. Her foot slipped in a rut of the muddy track. She was wearing her favourite boots. They were a pleasing shade of toffee, and soft as butter. She glanced down ruefully at the splattered leather. She wasn't sure they would stand up to this.

Trevor Shoesmith's home had no curtains visible in the windows. It gave the farmhouse a blank, derelict look. A police car was parked at an angle in front of the door, and beyond it, a white RSPCA van. There was no one in sight. No barking dogs. No movement.

"I told the PC to be here. Where the devil is he?" muttered Ben, his face grim. The five o'clock shadow along his jawline was stark against his skin. He picked up the pace.

The front door's paint had once been ox-blood red but now,

cracked and peeling, it had an unhealthy whitish bloom. Ben stopped short. Faith almost ran into the back of him. Instinctively, he put out an arm to hold her back. There were stains on the concrete step disappearing into the patchy gravelled earth beyond. Ben crouched down. He touched the ground lightly. He stood up, the tips of his fingers smudged red.

"Blood – or looks like. Fairly recent." He stepped around the stains, pulling on a fresh pair of latex gloves. "Careful of those." The tone of his voice had changed: calmer, authoritative. Faith's senses clicked into a higher state of alert.

He turned the door handle. The door wasn't locked.

The front door opened into a kitchen. No hallway. The light was dim. Faith received the impression of shades of sadness; no true colour anywhere. The furniture seemed sparse and utilitarian. A table, a few chairs, and a dirty Rayburn stove in the old chimney nook, its top encrusted with the charred remains of ancient spills. By it stood an old Windsor chair with a dog basket at its feet. Some traces of quality gleamed out in the line of the chair's curved oak back and legs, visible from under the drape of a plaid blanket and the dirty blue woollen shawl thrown over it. In the basket, old clothes and newspapers formed a nest. Newspapers lay everywhere: in the basket, littering the table and on the floor, sheets trampled with mud and dirt and less savoury stains.

They found other spurts and dashes of blood.

"What went on here?" Her own voice sounded startlingly vivid to Faith in the dank silence of the room.

Ben just grunted. "There's more here." He bent over the chair, picking up a corner of the plaid cloth: a dark, stiff stain.

"It's soaked and dried. Some time ago." He cocked his head, contemplating the shape of the stain. "Might have been wrapped round something?"

Faith joined him, noticing the roughly conical shape, maybe five inches high and broader at its base.

"A forearm, a wrist?" she suggested.

"Perhaps."

That corner stank. Beneath the matted dog hair, traces of bile and excrement soiled the basket. The furniture, the dirt, the smell, the very walls seemed to seep an atmosphere of despair. A sudden urgency to get out into the full light gripped Faith.

Footsteps crunched on gravel and a shadow passed the window.

"Inspector Shorter?" a man's voice called from outside.

A uniformed policeman appeared in the doorway carrying his helmet: a middle-aged man, heavy set and greying. His cheeks were flushed.

"Where've you been, constable?" Ben barked.

"Hanson. Jim Hanson, sir."

"I thought you had orders to meet me here, at the house?"

"Ran into two RSPCA officers as I arrived. They requested my assistance."

"And why was that? For God's sake, mind your feet!"

The constable skipped back a step and looked down bemusedly at his feet. He had scuffed the stain by the door.

"Get some tape and mark that area!" Ben's voice had the force of a blow. The constable didn't move.

"Well?" Ben demanded.

Jim Hanson eyed Faith, uncertainly.

"There's something you should see in the barn, sir," he said earnestly. Ben scrutinized his face.

"Now?"

"Yes sir."

"Lead on."

Jim Hanson set off around the corner of the house, then he hesitated.

"Perhaps the lady would prefer to stay here."

"Nonsense," Faith said briskly. "There's no need for that. I'm Faith Morgan, Reverend Morgan." She was glad to be wearing her clerical uniform. Police, firefighters, the medical profession, they were all inclined to give dog collars professional courtesy. Just another one of the emergency services. "I am taking over at St James's."

Jim seemed too preoccupied to want to make an issue of it. He took his cue from Ben, and she followed after them unhindered.

They rounded the corner of the house where a space opened out. Farm buildings clustered around an unkempt yard, grass growing through its cracked concrete surface. PC Hanson walked on, but Ben stopped. On the ground was a pool of blood. An arterial spray curved up the wall interrupted by a void. The PC turned back.

"Of course, there's that too," he said vaguely.

Ben looked at him. Hanson's attention was elsewhere. He was leading them towards a big shed made of aluminium siding within a steel frame. Ben glanced back at the stain as he followed on. Faith gave the blood a wide berth, noting that some of it was smudged and dragged as if someone had slipped in it – or even sat down in it. Across the uneven surface of the yard she noticed a distinct trail of drops and then a bloody jackknife. It lay in a groove of a concrete slab near a drain. Whoever had dropped it had made no attempt to conceal it. She pointed it out to Ben. He grunted.

The tall sliding doors were open a few feet. An RSPCA officer in a fluorescent jacket stood by them, smoking, his eyes down. As she drew nearer, Faith saw that his hands were shaking.

There was movement in the gloom within. The flash of another fluorescent jacket.

Faith stepped over the threshold. Her eyes took a moment to adjust. The space was cavernous. A few bales of straw were stacked haphazardly. Some farm machinery was parked at the far end. There was a smell of mould among the mustiness, and something else. Something cloying and foul that caught in her throat.

A man hung from a central beam. His face was congested. There was no life left in him.

"Is it Trevor?" asked Faith.

Hanson nodded. "I warned you."

Shoesmith's neck was broken. His head tilted at an entirely

wrong angle. Alive he had been over six foot, and broad with it. He must have jumped from quite a height, Faith thought. She felt sick. She pushed her emotional self into a box and tried to think only with her rational mind.

A tower of bales stood a few feet from where the body hung. It listed precariously, the top bale jutting out, ready to fall. He must have prepared the rope and then jumped from the bales.

Ben was looking in the same direction.

"One bale higher and he might have lost his head," he commented.

Faith swallowed hard against the bile rising in her throat. The sleeves were rolled up to the elbow of the hanging man's stained shirt. Beneath, the big hands hung raw and bloody. Shoesmith's forearms were covered with cuts. Stripes of white scar and fresh seeping wounds running parallel to each other from elbow to wrist.

The second fluorescent jacket belonged to a solidly built, open-faced young woman with blonde hair scraped back into a ponytail. She looked dazed.

"What's your name?" Faith asked.

"Hannah," she replied.

"Faith."

"His dog," said Hannah. Her voice shook. She pointed to a sheepdog lying on a bale. Grey muzzled. Not young. It took her a moment to register what was odd about the picture. The fur beneath its head was clotted with blood. Its throat had been cut. The animal had been positioned with care, its muzzle on its paws, its head turned towards its master in a parody of life.

"Why did he do that?" Hannah said.

"Anyone find a note?" Ben asked Jim.

"Not here. Not so far," the PC replied.

"Make sure no one destroys that evidence out there – everyone walks the long way round." Ben leaned down for a closer look at the dog.

"The knife in the yard," Faith said.

Ben nodded. "Looks as if he killed the dog out there by the wall and carried it in here."

"Who found him?" Ben walked back to the body. He reached up and lifted a bloody forefinger briefly.

Jim jerked his head at Hannah. "RSPCA. Arrived ten, fifteen minutes ago to sort out the animals and found him then."

"Been dead longer than that," commented Ben. "Everyone out," he ordered and flipped open his phone. "Hanson, radio this in and get the techs out ASAP."

Faith took Hannah by the elbow.

"Come on," she said, her voice gentle. "Let's go outside."

Hannah looked back at the dog. "Do I just leave him?"

"For now."

Outside they kept to the walls. The two RSPCA officers huddled together, whispering. Faith stood apart in her own space. She tried to pray for the soul of Trevor Shoesmith. She believed in a merciful God. She had no fears about that. What stopped her was anger. It poisoned her thoughts; made them unclean.

He should have listened to her! This need not have happened! She was angry at Ben. Furious. So much so, she thought she must be shaking with it. She looked at her hands. They were steady.

Look at him.

He's probably on the phone. Process. Action. Deal with it. That's his way! went the rant in her head.

But Ben wasn't on the phone. He was standing alone, entirely still, concentrating on a spot on the ground. Compassion overwhelmed her. The anger dispelled like smoke on a breeze.

She went over to stand by him. He spoke without looking up.

"You called it."

She wanted to hug him, but they were in public; it wasn't appropriate to hug an inspector in full view of a pair of RSPCA officers.

"There was no way you could anticipate this."

His blue eyes were like searchlights, direct, unflinching. "No? You did."

"I could just have easily have been wrong. Between us, we've seen enough suicides. The journey to this point will have started a long time ago – just look at those cuts on his arms."

"I never saw those. He had sleeves down all the time." He shuddered as if to throw something off his skin.

"I know. I know you didn't." She caught herself reaching out towards him and pulled her hand back.

He straightened up, looking towards the barn.

"Peter's on his way." He glanced down at her. "What time was it that you saw Jessica Rose coming from here?"

"Around 11:15 a.m."

He checked his watch. "Must have happened around then."

Faith thought of Jessica Rose leaving the farmhouse carrying that brightly coloured beach bag. What had happened here? She felt disorientated and unfocused.

Ben looked over at the farmhouse. "I'll set things going here, but then I need to track down Jessica Rose." His phone rang.

"You'd better answer that," she said.

She needed to get away. She walked out of the desolate yard and down the track, the mud clinging to her boots.

CHAPTER
10

THE SCENE OF CRIME OFFICERS HAD LEFT the vestry door standing open. Faith walked through the still church into the nave. The paper bag with its contents had been removed from the pew. Someone had closed the piano lid. A residue of aluminium powder clouded its surface, the mess of fingerprints standing out under the dust like skeleton leaves.

It was peaceful in the nave. Faith crossed in front of the altar and sat down in one of the well-polished pews by a pillar. The light slanted down through the stained-glass windows and glanced on the panel patiently awaiting its restoration against the wall. The cracked glass lamb on its emerald green lawn smiled its enigmatic smile from the shadows.

What is there to smile about? That poor man! What kind of misery had driven Trevor Shoesmith to that barn?

Could he really have poisoned Alistair Ingram?

She tried to picture a living man coming down that muddy track towards the church with murder in his mind.

She couldn't visualize Trevor Shoesmith alive. All she saw was the grotesque, distorted husk of a man hanging in the barn.

Words from Psalm 121 unwound in her mind.

> *The Lord is thy keeper: the Lord is thy shade upon thy right hand.*

*The sun shall not smite thee by day, nor the moon by
   night.
The Lord shall preserve thee from all evil: he shall
   preserve thy soul.*

Dear Lord, have mercy on his soul.

The stillness grew around her and she was at its centre.

She heard a slight noise, and looked up to see Jessica Rose
enter from the vestry. Jessica approached the piano.

Faith stood up. The wooden pew creaked against the stone
flags and Jessica spun round with a little squeal of surprise.

"You!" she exclaimed.

"It's gone," Faith said. The last bit of colour drained from
Jessica's face.

"Gone?" She swallowed. "What's gone?"

"The bag you put in the piano. The police have it."

It was like watching a building shimmering under a
catastrophic explosion. Jessica held the pose for a second and then
she began to shake with suppressed sobs. Tears swelled her pretty
blue eyes and rolled down her cheeks.

Faith went up and put her arms around her. They stood
there awkwardly for a minute. Faith noticed for the first time
that Jessica was not a purely natural blonde. Rich honey-toned
highlights had been skilfully added. Faith wondered briefly what
her real colour was.

"Suppose you tell me about it," she said aloud.

She could feel each of Jessica's sobs in her own chest. Some
preparation for Holy Week, Faith thought – murder, suicide,
despair.

Well, Lent is about the true cost of sin.

Her eye was caught by a drying crescent of mud, bearing the
imprint of her heel, bang in the middle of one of the cream floor
tiles. Now see the dirt you've tracked in, she thought.

"Let's sit down." She steered Jessica to the front pew. The
woman's breath was jerky, but she seemed a little calmer.

"I saw you this morning," Faith began in a quiet, soothing voice. Keep the tone non-committal, she told herself; non-judgmental – like a story recited to a child. "You came from the farm carrying something in a beach bag, and you left the church with it empty. The bag caught my attention. It looked so bright."

Jessica sniffed. "It's not mine. It was just to hand."

Faith found a paper handkerchief in a pocket and offered it. Jessica blew her nose.

"I wanted to warn Trevor after the meeting yesterday." Jessica twisted the tissue in her hands. "But she was there, outside the church hall." The long lashes fluttered. Her eyes were sapphire blue under the tears.

"Pat," said Faith.

Jessica nodded. "She lives in one of the cottages on the green. She's always looking out. I didn't dare."

The houses overlooking the green were exquisite eighteenth-century cottages, the type rapidly becoming weekend additions to the property portfolios of wealthy London bankers. Pat must be well off, Faith thought, absently wondering where the money came from. She refocused her attention on the woman before her.

Jessica gazed towards the light of the outside world streaming through the open vestry door. Her words came out slowly.

"I saw the police cars. They're up at the farm."

Does she know Trevor is dead? Faith wondered. Be still and see what she has to say.

"Is that why you came here?" she asked.

"I thought I should move it."

"What made you bring the pesticide here in the first place?"

"I don't know." Jessica looked at her wonderingly. Her mascara had smudged, accentuating the shadows under her eyes. "I had to hide it somewhere safe, and I didn't want to be seen carrying it about," she said simply. She seemed comfortable that Faith held the authority in that space – all-knowing, reassuring.

It's the dog collar that does it, thought Faith.

"I didn't sleep a wink all last night, worrying about poor Trevor. He didn't have anything to do with…" Jessica broke off, the tears welling up again as they both looked towards the altar where Alistair Ingram breathed his last.

Faith held her hand and squeezed it. Jessica took a deep breath.

"Trevor's not been well. He gets so low. And lately with his dog – Barney – he's been so sick. Well, he was just too old. Trevor loved that dog."

Past tense. Does she know? Faith thought.

"So Trevor was upset about his dog?" she prompted.

Jessica's eyes flickered, but she went on as if Faith hadn't spoken.

"I went to see Trevor this morning. I knew Pat would be away by ten. There's a Country Ladies' club outing to Mottisford Abbey Garden," she added unexpectedly, almost as if they were having a normal conversation.

Over Jessica's shoulder, Faith caught sight of a scene of crime officer standing looking in on them from the vestry door. The man met her eyes with a quizzical look. She shook her head in a faint negative. The man retreated, walking softly.

"How did you find him – Trevor?" Faith thought of the dog laid out on the bale of rotting straw. "Had something happened to Barney?"

Jessica's face crumpled. "Barney was dying. Trevor had never moved all night. Right there in the kitchen. He was so upset." She turned her face away.

That's not what she was going to say, thought Faith. I wonder what's been edited out.

"That dog's been in pain for weeks." Jessica's words came more rapidly now. "You could see it in the way he breathed, and he hadn't been eating. Last week the vet told Trevor he must be put down, but Trevor couldn't do it. Barney was the last one bred from a bitch he bought the year his mother died. He was his last family. And then all this happened."

Jessica squeezed her eyes shut, blocking out the view of the altar before them. She drew in a sharp breath. "He'd been doing so much better!" Her hands were balled in tight fists. "Then the police – all the questions…"

Jessica reached out and gripped her arm with such unexpected force that Faith flinched.

"I encouraged him to buy the pesticide! I told him, start small; start on a little patch by the house. A corner of his mother's garden. Make it grow again…" The pace of her words accelerated, her face flushed and fat tears ran down Jessica's face, her breath coming short.

"Shhh," Faith tried to soothe her. Much more of this and there would no getting any sense out of her.

"So you went to see Trevor this morning, because of what Fred said to us at the church hall meeting," prompted Faith.

Jessica Rose nodded, her face down. She let go of Faith's arm and slumped against the pew.

"You said Trevor was upset about his dog. How upset?" Jessica shifted in her seat until she had almost turned her back. Faith's voice was insistent. "How upset was he, Jessica? Did you think he was a danger to himself?"

Jessica looked up, her eyes pleading. "I took the pesticide," she said in a small voice. "I thought if the tin was gone, then he couldn't get in trouble."

Faith was caught out by a sudden kick of anger. Jessica was a grown woman, not a child!

"You didn't just leave him?" she exclaimed. She heard the force of the indignation in her own voice, and made an effort to speak more calmly. "If you really thought he was likely to hurt himself – if he was that bad, surely he needed professional help?"

"I tried to help him!" Jessica was crying again. "From the beginning, I tried! But he wouldn't let me tell. I had no right…" Jessica imprisoned her hands between her knees, her arms tense. She rocked a little, back and forth. "We're not related. I haven't known him that long. Trevor's a very private man."

Her distress was infectious. Faith felt her own eyes tearing in sympathy. But *there's more*, said a cool, detached voice in her head. *Jessica Rose is hiding something she feels guilty about – and it's not just that tin of pesticide. All that blood in the kitchen – it wasn't put there in the first few minutes after she'd left.*

"When you saw Trevor this morning in his kitchen, what happened?"

Jessica's eyes were fixed straight ahead, on the altar.

"He died here," she said, her voice a whisper in the silence.

Who was she talking about? Faith glanced up at the altar. Did she mean that the chain of circumstances that led to Trevor's death began here?

Alistair Ingram had died here, behind the altar.

Jessica closed her eyes.

Faith felt a hand on her shoulder. Ben slipped into the pew behind them. She had been concentrating so hard that she hadn't seen him come in. She felt his presence, solid at her back.

Jessica didn't move. Faith touched her arm and she opened her eyes.

"Jessica, this is Inspector Shorter. He is with the police."

"Mrs Rose," said Ben in a matter-of-fact voice. Jessica barely acknowledged him. "I've just come from the Shoesmith farm. I have a couple of questions about your visit there this morning."

Peter was standing by the door holding a notebook. Jessica's eyes were fixed on Faith. She looked at Ben, apparently uncertain what to do.

"Suppose you see if you can find us a cup of tea?" Ben said. Faith bridled. She wasn't his servant! She bit her tongue. He held her look and gave a faint jerk of his head towards the door.

It was his investigation and he had the authority. Besides, she had the feeling that Jessica had said as much as she was going to for the time being. She rose. Jessica looked after her longingly.

"I'll be right back," Faith reassured her.

She made for the vicarage, a few yards away through the lime trees. Don was standing in the garden outside the kitchen, watching the activity at Trevor Shoesmith's farm. Two more police cars had arrived, and an ambulance.

"What's up at the Shoesmith place?" he asked without preamble.

"Shoesmith's hung himself." The brutality of the statement caught her by surprise. She hadn't meant to say it right out like that.

Don looked startled. He was thoughtful for a moment, then he snapped out of it. "Do you want me for something?"

"Tea. I was hoping I could beg four mugs of tea." She looked back. "To take to the church. Inspector Shorter and his sergeant are interviewing Jessica Rose in there."

"No problem." Don led the way into the kitchen.

"Jessica Rose, you say," he said, setting out mugs and popping a tea bag in each. "How's she doing?" The kettle boiled.

He's not questioning why she's there, thought Faith.

"Not great." Faith poured the boiling water into the cups.

"I don't suppose she is," he grunted. "Two admirers dead in a week. That woman's toxic."

She slopped hot water over the edge of the mug. It pooled on the countertop and ran in a rivulet towards the edge.

"What?" Now it was her voice that had the hysterical edge.

Don looked down at her with a sly expression.

"Oops!" He leaned over to grab a cloth from the sink, and mopped up the spill.

"None of that!" She waved his hand aside. "This is serious. Jessica and your father?"

"I'm surprised one of the Worthy worthies hasn't dropped you the hint yet. They're slipping. Mind you, the lovebirds were very careful." He slid her a speculative look under his long lashes. "Shocked? They were both single, you know."

Faith thought about it. No, she wasn't shocked. She saw the distinguished-looking Alistair Ingram as he was when alive, and then Jessica sitting on the floor by the body, rocking and holding the dead man's hand. It was obvious! How had she missed it?

"Why was it such a secret?"

"Dad liked to be private about personal affairs. She's divorced. Then there's that priest/parishioner thing. It's a bit like a doctor getting it on with a patient."

"Hardly!" For heaven's sake, vicars were human beings too.

Don cocked his head at her. "Oh, come on! In a village like this? Blonde divorcee snags vicar? The old biddies would be in uproar."

"Did the bishop know?"

"Dad had a few private meetings up at the bishop's house."

She thought of Bishop Anthony. She would have guessed he was quite traditional about such affairs, but she wasn't sure. A widower and a divorcee. Personally she couldn't see anything wrong in that – as long as the widower hadn't been involved in the collapse of the divorcee's previous marriage. She wondered why the bishop hadn't mentioned Ingram's relationship, and then dismissed the thought. Why on earth should he blab to her? She wasn't the police. She had to keep reminding herself of that these days.

"Was that why your father was retiring?" She asked.

Don shrugged. "Part of it. Dad was full of his new life ahead. Just him and the new woman." Bitterness threaded through his words, like concealed razor wire. "He couldn't wait."

Faith picked up the tray. "I've got to get back now, but we'll talk about this."

She searched his handsome face. Just how angry had he been about his father's choice? He met her gaze blandly.

She put the tray into his hands.

"You can make yourself useful."

He took the tray and they walked in silence across the garden and along the path through the lime trees.

"He loved her," Don said quietly. "To be honest, I think they loved each other."

"And what about Trevor Shoesmith?"

"What about him?"

"Did you know that they were friends – Jessica and Trevor?"

"You've got a dirty mind," he chided, flicking a glance at her dog collar with a sly grin. "Nah. It wasn't like that. I think she was just doing good works."

He stopped short, a few feet from the vestry door. Faith glanced up and was surprised by his tense expression.

"I'm not going in there," he said flatly.

Faith took the tray from him.

"You don't have to," she said.

He began to move away, backing in the direction they'd come. His usual confidence clicked into place as if it had never faltered.

"But come see me after, eh? Let me know what's going on. I'll make you a sandwich," he ended with a wave.

Faith nodded a vague acknowledgment, and carried the tray into the church.

Ben greeted the tea with barely suppressed frustration. Jessica was wan and silent. There was a faintly stubborn look about her mouth. He can't have brought up Trevor's suicide yet, then, thought Faith. She felt a twinge of guilt at being party to such a deception. She resumed her seat next to Jessica on the pew. Behind them, Ben sat back. She took the movement as tacit approval.

"Jessica," she said, handing her a mug, "I was wondering why you didn't mention your relationship with Alistair Ingram."

All credit to Ben. He didn't move a muscle. Jessica, on the other hand, blushed like a guilty teenager.

"Well, I…" She wouldn't meet Faith's eye.

Faith took a sip of tea. "Was it a serious relationship?" she enquired conversationally. Behind her, she heard Ben exhale brusquely through his nose. Jessica looked at Faith, shocked, as if she hadn't expected such a query from a vicar.

"Of course! We were engaged to be married." A tear rolled down her cheek. She wiped it away with the back of her hand.

"Alistair thought it was best he was retired before we made it public. We were in love." Her voice was reverent. "He was the most wonderful man I have ever known. And he's gone."

There was such loss in that small phrase. Faith cleared her throat. She felt filthy, prying like this, but she had to ask.

"Did Don know of the engagement?"

"Alistair was going to tell him that day – that morning."

Why hadn't Don mentioned the engagement? Perhaps his father died before he could broach the subject. Faith thought of her first glimpse of Don storming away from his father, and his father reaching out to him from the vestry door. She wondered about a son who had lost his mother and then, in his eyes, lost his father to the church. Just how angry might such a son have been to learn that that father was prepared to give up the church that had appeared to mean so much more to him than his surviving family, for this woman?

She saw Don stopping short at the vestry door just a few moments ago. *I'm not going in there.*

"How about Trevor Shoesmith?" Faith started at the sound of Ben's voice. She had almost forgotten he was there.

"Trevor?" Jessica repeated. She seemed bemused.

"Didn't he fancy himself in love with you, too?"

Ben could have phrased that more tactfully! Faith glared at him behind Jessica's back. He rolled his eyes at her in an entirely unprofessional way as he felt in his pocket. He took out a letter in a plastic evidence bag, and read:

"*I am sitting here thinking of the barn and the feel of your hair against my skin. Jessica, you know what you are to me – everything. In your arms I can be all those things you say I can.*"

Faith felt like a pervert. She wished she was anywhere else but sitting there in that pew. Ben seemed entirely unaffected by what he was doing. He was watching Jessica. She was rigid.

"Were you having a relationship with Mr Shoesmith?" asked Ben.

"No!" Jessica was indignant. "It was nothing like that."

"No?" Ben looked down at the letter in its plastic bag. "So what did happen... in the barn?"

Jessica tucked a strand of her hair behind an ear and squirmed in her seat. "It was one time... Trevor told me some things about his past; he got upset; I tried to comfort him. It was a tender moment – but not passionate," she said emphatically, and shook her head once. "I didn't feel that way about Trevor."

"Did you tell him that?" Ben's voice was sarcastic.

"Oh yes, I did. I did tell him." Jessica's eyes filled with tears again.

"But he hadn't given up his hopes?"

She raised a small fist to her mouth. "No," she said, and began to sob.

Faith put her arms around her and held her as she cried. Behind them, Ben sat back relaxed, one arm stretched out along the pew back, watching and waiting. She tried to ignore him.

"This morning," Faith spoke softly, "what happened? Why did you leave him?"

Jessica's voice was clogged with tears. "He'd started again," she said.

"Started again?"

Leaning into her like a child, with one hand Jessica drew a vague slicing gesture across her arm just below the elbow.

"Trevor would cut himself?" asked Faith.

The blonde head nodded once, like a puppet. "He'd been doing it off and on for years, I think. I've been trying to help him." Jessica rummaged around in a pocket and brought out another handkerchief.

"So you did your best," Faith's voice was gentle.

Again the puppet nod. "I did my best." She blew her nose.

Jessica lifted her head. She turned to look back at Ben. "How did you get that letter?"

He looked back at her in silence.

"Where's Trevor?" Jessica asked. She blinked twice, then gave a tiny shake of her head. "He's dead, isn't he?"

"Yes," said Ben.

"I am so sorry, Jessica." Faith wished words weren't so inadequate. She wondered how Ben could sit there so unmoved. Now Jessica's beautiful eyes, full of tears, turned wildly to her.

"I left him!" Her voice was shrill. "I left him there this morning. I knew the state he was in and I left him!"

"Why did you leave?"

Jessica made a clumsy gesture in the direction of the letter Ben held, and her hand hit the pew hard. She didn't even flinch.

"Because of that. Oh, I knew he had feelings for me! I thought we'd had that out months ago – I made it clear: we were just friends, that was all. He said he understood. But then, this morning he got so worked up – pleading with me. He said he was doing it for me! What was he trying to prove? The blood! It was disgusting. I knew he'd had times like this before. He told me once it was a release. A release? How could it be a release?" She was rocking back and forth now, with an intensity Faith found worrying. Her phrases came out in an odd, mechanical rhythm. "I was making it worse. I had to leave – but I took the pesticide, in case…"

"In case he used it on himself?" Faith asked, hoping to cut into her mounting hysteria.

Jessica nodded, her lips compressed, her jaw rigid.

"And what did Trevor think of your relationship with Alistair Ingram?" Ben's voice intruded. Faith glared at him. His question galvanized Jessica. She swung to face him.

"Trevor was a good and kind man!" she howled at him. "He *never* hurt anyone but himself!" She folded herself up as if she wanted to disappear and began to rock, moaning in a way that made the hairs stand up on the back of Faith's neck.

CHAPTER

FAITH FELT WRUNG OUT. SHE SAT in her car outside her sister's house, too tired to get out. It was exhausting, dealing so intimately with misery and death.

They'd had to call a doctor to Jessica. He'd given her a sedative. Faith had seen her home, limp and passive, to her cottage in a hamlet outside Little Worthy. Jessica's neighbour, Di, a primary school teacher with three grown-up children, had offered to stay with her. Together they had put her to bed in her low-eaved room with its embroidered linen and limewashed French furniture. In the sunny room Jessica's head lay on the freshly laundered pillow, her face blotchy with tears, clutching the bedclothes under her chin like a child.

Despite everything, Faith had made her meeting with the rural dean on time. Life goes on. Canon Matthews had been sympathetic, but businesslike. They had discussed plans for Alistair Ingram's funeral that coming Friday. The bishop would take it. It would be a public affair. The press had got wind of the story. Faith wondered how Don was feeling about the church assuming charge of Alistair Ingram's final farewell as if he belonged to them, his son no more than a mourner. She tried to raise this with the rural dean, but Canon Matthews merely looked wise and said something about anger being a natural stage of bereavement. Faith let it drop for the time being: perhaps she should speak to the bishop himself. Canon Matthews had frowned at her idea of physically cleaning the church alongside her parishioners, asking if there wasn't a regular cleaning rota. Faith had said that wasn't quite the point and he had shrugged, admitting it might serve some "symbolic" function.

Faith didn't want to go into her sister's house. Ruth lived in a modern close. Ten properties arranged in a neat horseshoe like some blow-moulded Barbie set, each house so like the next, as if individual humanity was an embarrassment – something to be hidden from the neighbours. Given the fallout she had been dealing with of late, it occurred to Faith that perhaps someone had a point.

She thought longingly of her own Birmingham flat with its high ceilings and familiar clutter. She imagined herself coming home. She would kick off her shoes and make herself a mug of tea and read her post at the bleached pine table. Later she might grill herself some chicken, toss a salad and eat in front of the TV. No questions. No explanations. No making conversation. Just quiet.

The plastic-coated front door opened and Ruth stood there shoeless in her work suit. She looked cross.

"So – are you coming in or what?" she yelled. "You've been sitting out there for ages!"

Faith forced a smile and obediently gathered up her things.

"You won't believe the day I've had," said Ruth, as she led the way down the hall.

"Shall I make us some tea?"

"You know what? I fancy a sherry."

Faith sighed internally. Ruth was in the mood for a bit of sisterly commiseration.

"Maybe I'll stick to tea."

"Oh, don't say that! I can't drink alone with you sipping tea."

"Don't let me stop you."

"It's not as if I'm a drinker," Ruth said belligerently. Faith saw that her participation in the sherry drinking had become a point of principle.

"Come on. I have had a pig of a day." Ruth marched to the kitchen and got out two glasses and a bottle of sweet white wine. "There's this young career woman type they've taken on to run some stupid 'vision' committee – a waste of money if ever I saw one." Ruth worked as an administrator at the county council offices in Winchester. "She comes swanning in at ten to three and demands I get this typing done on the double because she wants it at the printers at four. The cheek of it! Thinks she can just come in and give me orders without a thought to the system."

"Perhaps if she's new she doesn't know the system," offered Faith mildly, sipping her wine and longing for tea.

Ruth snorted derisively. "Well, I told her, I am the chief executive's assistant, and I have plenty of jobs of my own, thank you. Put it on the pile for the juniors and maybe someone will get round to it next week. Ha!" Ruth exclaimed with bitter self-satisfaction.

Faith leaned back in her chair and stretched her neck.

"What's up with you?" demanded Ruth.

"Oh, just a long day."

"Seen much of Ben?" Her sister's eyes turned beady.

"A bit." Faith got up and headed towards the kitchen. "What do you fancy to eat? I think I should cook for you tonight."

"Check the fridge." Ruth followed her, glass in hand, crowding her in the tiny kitchen. "So, spill. How was it? How are you two getting along?"

It was as if a perished rubber band gave way somewhere deep inside.

"We found a man hanging in a barn," Faith stated. "Then we spent an unpleasant couple of hours interrogating the person closest to the suicide. We had to call the doctor. It wasn't what you'd call romantic."

She shouldn't have let it out like that. It was as if she had spat out something toxic, polluting the mundane familiarity of that kitchen. Ruth stared at her, perplexed and uncertain. Faith could see she didn't know what to say. Who would?

"I'm sorry," Ruth said at last.

"Me, too."

Ruth rubbed her arm and patted it. "More wine?" she said, with a nervous half-giggle.

"Actually, I prefer tea."

"So who was the suicide?" Ruth said, putting on the kettle.

"Trevor Shoesmith."

Her sister swung round to face her. "No! Oh, Mum will be upset."

I'm not sure why, Faith thought. Mum hadn't seen Trevor for years. These exclamations people made on the news of death – they were so insufficient; conventional phrases obscuring the reality that no words could build a bridge into the misery of those truly caught up in the loss. Faith curled up inside at the thought of all the gasping expressions of sympathy there would be from strangers about Trevor Shoesmith's suicide. Ghoulishness masquerading as concern!

You *are* in a bad mood, commented a detached voice in the back of her head.

"Well, at least Ben was there," she heard her sister say.

Faith closed her eyes. When faced with the unknowable, harp on the familiar. It is only human nature. Be charitable.

"I just don't see why you are being so silly about him!" Ruth was picking up speed now that she was back on familiar territory. "Ben's clearly still interested – although why, after the way you've treated him, I don't know. It's not as if you've got any other prospects. And now you're local. You're not getting any younger!"

"Roo – not now. OK?" Faith pleaded. "Have mercy!"

The phone rang.

"I'm going to have a bath," said her sister curtly. "You can answer that." She flounced up the stairs.

Faith answered the phone. "Yes?" she snapped.

"You're in a good mood," said Ben's voice in her ear.

"The world's such a glorious place!" she quipped bitterly.

"Mmm. Tough day."

"That it was."

The electricity of the open line crackled between them.

"Thought I would check on how you left Mrs Rose," he said.

"For heaven's sake! She was numb with shock – she couldn't even speak coherently." The words tumbled out with a violence that caught Faith by surprise. "She wasn't in any condition to make any further confessions, and I wasn't in the mood to pry." After all they had witnessed that day, he was still expecting her to spy for him!

"That's not what I meant and you know it," responded Ben in a flat voice.

"I'm sorry." She wasn't being fair. Faith sat down on the bottom stair and propped herself up against the café au lait-painted wall. She began again in a more reasonable tone. "She was exhausted. We put her to bed. The neighbour's keeping an eye on her."

"I've alerted victim services. They're sending someone to check on her tomorrow."

"Good."

Again the silence stretched out between them. It was dim on the stairs. Ruth was trying to save electricity.

"Did you find a suicide note?"

"Under the dog."

Faith had a brief mental image. "That's unpleasant."

"Mmm. Bit of a mess."

"What did it say?"

"Brief and not very helpful. It's addressed to Jessica."

"And says?"

"I loved you. I'm sorry," he said.

"Meaning I'm sorry I loved you?"

"More – I loved you – stop – I'm sorry – stop. Two distinct sentiments."

Faith shrugged. "Still, the impact's the same. Guilt trip placed firmly on Jessica."

"Maybe he didn't even put them together in his own head – who can tell," Ben said philosophically. Faith knew such sidetracks didn't interest him.

"Suicide is such a miserable act." She knew it was a pointless statement, but the waste made her cross. "It inflicts such open-ended guilt on those left behind."

"Maybe that is the suicide's point."

"The ultimate passive-aggressive revenge."

"Pointless since you're not there to enjoy it." He paused. She heard the shift in his voice. "It's just been confirmed. Trevor Shoesmith had an alibi for Ingram's death."

He waited as if he expected her to crow, or at least offer an "I told you so", but she just felt exhaustingly sad.

"Where was he?"

"We have witnesses that put him in a pub in a neighbouring village on Saturday night. He got so plastered a friend gave him a bed for the night."

"And the friend's reliable?"

"A respected farmer and his wife." Ben sounded tired. "According to them, Shoesmith was out of it. He didn't wake up until late morning on Sunday – after Ingram was already dead."

So Trevor Shoesmith was harried in his final days for nothing – all because she had repeated gossip to Ben.

"So you're not going say it?" Ben prompted.

"Would it make you feel better if I did?"

Ben grunted. The noise of water filling the bath upstairs was loud in the still hall. Ruth went into the bathroom and closed the door.

"So it's back to basics," Ben said.

Let's move on. Ben Shorter has a murderer to catch.

She pulled herself up. It was true; that was his job. And hers was to find God in the midst of this tragedy, and serve the community of St James's.

"What've you got?" she heard herself ask. When they were

together, they would always do this at the end of the day – discuss the case in hand, go over things. Old habits were hard to break. "When was the poison put in the wine?"

She heard a rustle down the line. She imagined Ben leaning back in his chair, stretching out his long legs as he ordered his thoughts.

"Well, they had an eight o'clock communion service that morning. No problems there. Mr Partridge, the churchwarden, says he poured the wine out into that carafe thing…"

"The cruet," Faith supplied.

"Whatever – he opened a new bottle for that first service. We've checked the bottle. Nothing there. After the eight o'clock service, they'd run low and Mr Partridge says the vicar refilled the *cruet*," Ben paused ironically to emphasize his mastery of the term. Alone in Ruth's hall, Faith smiled. "It was left on that side table by the altar ready for the next service. When pushed, Mr Partridge admitted he might have left the vestry unlocked when he went home for a snack between the services – his usual practice, I am told."

"So the poison was put in the cruet after the wine was decanted?"

"Yes."

"What sort of time?"

"Best guess the wine was left unattended for ten, fifteen minutes between the church emptying after the eight o'clock service and people arriving for the ten o'clock."

Faith visualized the vestry and the approach from the vicarage screened by the lime trees, the open field beyond the stone wall. That offered the most discreet access. Slip across the short cut from the lane by Shoesmith's farm and behind the church. Someone could conceal themselves behind that stone wall and wait opposite the vestry door for the coast to be clear. The front of the church was overlooked from too many points – there was a good chance that passers-by or people in the houses across the green would spot somebody approaching that way.

"The poisoner would have to be pretty confident," she commented. "I mean, there is always a chance that one of the churchwardens would come in early, or the vicar."

"Puts the focus on people who had a reason to be there – the churchwardens?" said Ben.

Faith thought of Fred Partridge and Pat Montesque. They were both so ordinary and normal-looking.

"That's insane."

"Is it? Fred Partridge is a farmer's merchant. He sells the stuff that killed the vicar."

"Are you sure? I mean, I can see he would carry pesticide, but can you identify the particular pesticide used?"

"Down to brand and batch. The brand is common enough, but it's only sold through agricultural suppliers – and Partridge is on the list of local stockists. As for batch – apparently each lot has some distinguishable marker – the lab's made an ID. I'm waiting for the manufacturers to come back with a list of who was supplied with that particular batch. Then we'll have something to run down."

Faith thought of Fred's homely, open face. "But what could be his motive?"

"Don't know. But we might dig something up," he said. "Wasn't it good old Fred who pointed the finger at Trevor?" Ben's question sidled in, crab-like.

Could she possibly have misread Fred? She hated this. She prided herself on her ability to weigh up people, but poisoning was such a sneaking way of death. It infected the whole community; anyone could be a suspect. All it took was a good actor, or someone delusional. Pat Montesque's round, powdered face sprang to mind. *She lives in one of the houses across the green and Jessica's afraid of her.* Not in that way! Don't be ridiculous!

Ben's voice intruded, breaking into her thoughts.

"You might be half-right though. What if the poisoner *is* insane – just someone with a grudge against the church, or the rite, or heard a voice. But none of that helps us. Whoever it was, he or she had good luck…"

"Hardly luck!" Faith interrupted.

Ben went on as if she hadn't spoken: "… the amount Ingram consumed in that wine shouldn't have killed him, except for his dodgy heart."

"You think it was an accident? That the poisoner didn't mean to kill? Or that the poisoner knew about Ingram's heart condition?" Faith got up and took the phone into the kitchen. She picked up her tea, cradling the handset in the crook of her neck.

"We'll have to ask him or her – when we find them."

As she cuddled the receiver close to her ear, his voice was startlingly intimate. She imagined Ben's mouth close to the receiver at the other end of the line. When *we* find them.

"One thing that's been bothering me," she said.

"Mmm?"

"Why did Alistair Ingram drink that wine? The smell was so wrong."

"All pesticide's manufactured with a stench factor – so I'm told," he said.

"Right. I noticed it in the stain on the altar cloth – it was partly why I didn't try mouth-to-mouth. It makes me wonder, could *Ingram* have committed suicide?"

"I thought he was too much of a man of God to do such a thing?" Ben taunted.

"And I thought you didn't take me seriously," she quipped back.

Ben laughed. "Maybe we're being too complicated. Like most Englishmen, Ingram went ahead, not wanting to make a fuss – after all, why should he imagine he's going to be poisoned?"

"You do tend to get rather caught up in the meaning – it is such a powerful moment," agreed Faith, thinking of her own feelings when she celebrated the Eucharist. She stopped abruptly. The sense of intimacy she had been feeling between them fractured. Ben didn't understand the reality she experienced through her faith. He didn't even recognize its existence. That was the gulf between them.

"Suicide would be convenient, but… no note," Ben forged on. Facts were always his defence. "No evidence he was anything but looking forward to his retirement. He had money in the bank, a new lady friend and no skeletons in the closet that we can find. Suicide doesn't fit."

She went back to the hall and sat down again on the bottom step. Her tea had gone cold. On the floor above, she heard Ruth come out of the bathroom and cross into her bedroom. Faith realized they had been talking for nearly twenty minutes.

"You always were good to talk to," he said. There was an unexpected tentativeness in his voice. "I miss this."

The simple words were like a hook in her chest. But she couldn't go back. It had cost too much to get herself to this place.

"Remind me," he said. "Just why did we break up?"

"Let's not do this," she said in a rush. "I know we've been flung together over this case, but can't we be civilized about it?"

"Civilized?"

She wished she had used better words.

"You have your job to do and I have mine – I have been getting too caught up in this…"

Ruth came down the stairs, her eyes averted. She stepped over Faith with a smug expression.

"I have to go," Faith said. "I'm cooking tonight."

"Where are you tomorrow?"

She had to put a stop to this.

"I have a deanery meeting at the cathedral." She wasn't going to admit to him that it would only last a couple of hours. The pause lengthened between them.

"OK." Ben's voice was steely. "You're doing your God thing."

"Good luck with…" she began.

Ben broke the connection.

She put the receiver back down carefully on the cradle. Ruth looked out from the kitchen.

"You don't have to cut the call short just because I'm here. I won't eavesdrop," she said mendaciously.

"We were just discussing the… his case."

"Just like old times," Ruth commented.

Faith went to the fridge. She was too old for this big sister act.

They needed to go shopping. The fridge was almost bare. There were eggs, though, and half a packet of tired-looking ham.

"How about a ham omelette?"

Ruth faced her. Her mouth was set in a mulish line that Faith recognized of old. There was no doing anything about it. Her sister was going to speak her mind.

"I think you are being dishonest," Ruth said. "You made such a fuss about leaving the police for the church, and now you're playing footsie with Ben over this murder. You're not being fair to him. If you are the *Reverend* Faith Morgan," the emphasis was sarcastic, "then it's really none of your business. He's not ringing you up for your expert advice."

Ruth's words stung. What was it, again, about family? Why was it family was supposed to be such a good thing?

Because they know you.

There were five wizened mushrooms rolling around in the vegetable drawer. "A ham and mushroom omelette?" Faith suggested.

Ruth gave up in disgust. "You know, it's time you grew up," she said, heading for the phone. "I'm going to order pizza."

Faith gazed at the bare fridge, the light reflecting off its white space. Would it were big enough to climb inside and close the door. Oh, to step out of the world for a spell and put oneself on ice – it sounded restful.

But Ruth was right. She should grow up. She closed the door. She would put Ben and his case out of her mind and concentrate on her true calling: to be the best pastor she could be to the people of St James's, Little Worthy. Fred might be at the deanery meeting tomorrow. She would talk to him about gathering people for her church cleansing ceremony. She'd already pinned up a notice on the church gate, but it couldn't hurt for a local to spread the word.

She felt better. Then an unwelcome thought intruded.

How did she know she wouldn't be talking to Alistair Ingram's murderer?

CHAPTER
12

STEADY RAIN BLURRED THE GLASS. It transformed the neat confines of her blue car into a cosy private world, lulled by the sibilant hush of the water spray thrown up by the tyres outside. The traffic was slow into town. Bishop Anthony was expected to drop into the deanery meeting that morning. Faith hoped she might catch a word with him. The logical part of her brain asked what she could expect from him, but the rest of her longed for some authoritative advice: *This* is how a priest behaves when the law is seeking a murderer among their congregation…

As she tucked her car into one of the parking slots by Church House, she noticed an estate car bearing the logo of the local TV station. Beyond it stood the battered red Escort she had seen before on the green in Little Worthy. Journalists. Damn.

She unfurled the big black umbrella she kept on the back seat. Through a window she saw the diocesan press officer, George Casey, caught in the glare of a camera light. Fortunately the deanery meeting was being held across the way. There was no need for her to be spotted. It seemed, so far, that she hadn't been identified as Alistair Ingram's successor. Keeping her head down under the violet light of the umbrella's deep bell, she picked her way across the rain-glossed tarmac, trying not to get her shoes too wet. There was nothing worse than spending a morning in a poorly heated hall with soggy feet.

She'd arrived half an hour early. There was no one in the hall apart from a couple of caterers setting out cups for the welcome coffee. They glanced at her impatiently as if she were harrying them. She decided to take a stroll.

The Close felt peaceful. The rain had eased to a light drizzle. Moisture dripped off the trees onto empty paths, hitting her umbrella with the occasional satisfying *pop*. Across the expanse of grass, a solitary couple shrouded in bright plastic macs consulted a guidebook. Few visitors were so eager as to venture out first thing on a wet Wednesday morning in April.

The Close made a patchwork of the church's past. The thirteenth-century porch from the medieval St Swithun's priory sewn into the fabric of the deanery; the medieval half-hipped roof and timbered frame of the Pilgrims' Hall, and the Georgian façade of The Judges' Lodging – the encrustation of the centuries accumulated in the shadow of the great cathedral, that magnificent expression of medieval technology and faith.

Bones and relics… of what? she pondered. Did this survival tell of the authority of the church, or the endurance of faith?

Her eyes roamed over the bricks and mortar. She had known this place all her life. She felt proud of its beauty and history, but it wasn't this that had drawn her to the ministry. She had first found faith in faces; in people transformed by faith. She thought of the bereaved mother of a teenage knife victim she had met in her third year in the police force. She remembered the woman's sorrow, her flashes of wit; her extraordinary forgiveness and hope. That encounter ultimately led her to Canon Jonathan. Then he had caught her up with his engagement, his humanity – his purpose: and that had drawn her in.

Trevor Shoesmith's mottled face flashed before her, and she felt a moment of despair. Did her faith – did she herself – measure up to all this?

She heard running steps behind her and swung round. Beyond the bell of her umbrella, Fred Partridge came into view.

"I thought it was you!" he said, puffing a little. "I called from back there, but you can't have heard me. I am glad you were able to come today." He wore a waterproof jacket, but his head was bare. Drops of moisture beaded in the lamb curls that fringed his bald pate.

"I have read the papers," Faith assured him, "but I shall have to rely on you if anything needs to be said. I'm still finding my feet."

"You have been dumped in at the deep end!" he sympathized. "But you're doing a gallant job."

Gallant. Faith smiled. It was an appropriately "Fred word", she decided. She looked into his guileless, open face, and felt a surge of warmth towards him. Fred Partridge was a good man, she was sure of it. She noticed he was looking tired. He lacked his usual bounce.

"You found Trevor Shoesmith," he said abruptly. His plump forehead creased in worried lines.

"Yes."

"I feel terrible," he exclaimed. "I was the one who put the police onto him." His voice quavered and his eyes misted. Faith tucked a hand under his arm.

"Come over here. Let's sit for a moment." She steered him to a secluded bench off the line of the path.

They sat on the bench side by side. The rain had stopped. She collapsed her umbrella. Fred looked at the ground, struggling to compose himself. She reached over and took his hand. He squeezed back, hard.

"A shocking thing!" he said.

"Yes."

"Gossiping about that pesticide sale. I shouldn't have done it!" He shook his head furiously at himself. He was getting quite distressed.

"Fred," she spoke firmly. He looked at her. "Did you speak the truth? About the pesticide, I mean?"

Fred widened his eyes in surprise. "Yes," he replied. "I did."

"And we know pesticide was used to kill Alistair Ingram," she continued. "So I don't see what else you could have done."

"Are you sure?"

In a dim corner of her brain she was astonished by his trust in her authority. She considered his query. Yes. Funnily enough she felt sure of Fred's innocence: but less sure of her own.

"Besides, it was I who took the information to the police," she said out loud.

"Oh!" Fred's exclamation was reassuring. He patted their clasped hands with his free one. "You had to do that. And I am grateful. I am ashamed to have put it on you."

They looked out across the lush, damp grass. Fred still held her hand. Gently, she tried to extricate her fingers. He held on.

"There's something else," he said.

What now?

He looked down and released her hand suddenly, breaking the connection. His eyes searched the far reaches of the Close.

"Trevor Shoesmith wasn't the only one I supplied that pesticide to."

Good old Fred, pointing the finger again, Ben's voice said in her head.

"Oh?"

"He came to mind because it was that one time – he wasn't a regular customer."

"But now there is a regular customer that comes to mind?"

Fred gave a tortured grimace. He beat his hands against his thighs twice. "I don't know if I should mention it now…" He appealed to her. "Should I?"

It's not as if we've had a good track record so far, ran the commentary in her head. Who's he been selling to? Pat Montesque? Perhaps Pat uses it on her roses. She almost smiled openly at the thought.

"Perhaps if you just tell me," she suggested.

"The bishop's farm," he said in a burst. He paused, watching her reaction anxiously.

"The bishop's farm," she repeated slowly.

"It's just down the road. Bishop Anthony visits there often – but that's ridiculous; isn't it?" he queried.

She was confused. Then she remembered the tomatoes served at the bishop's lunch and light dawned. "The farm run by that charity – some acronym." She thought of squirrels. "ACORN? But I thought they were organic?"

Fred scratched his cheek. "They're having a bit of a tussle with young McIvor over that."

"McIvor?"

"Luke McIvor," Fred explained. "He's the land agent – in charge of all the diocesan properties. He won't let the ACORN lot go fully organic. There's been a pest problem in the area."

"So they've bought pesticide from you."

Fred nodded.

"And the same brand?"

He nodded again, his face a parody of solemnity.

But you're an agricultural supplier, she thought. You must sell loads of the stuff. She contemplated Fred's body language. Why mention that farm and the bishop himself? He seemed concerned but she couldn't discern anything else. "Well, I am sure you sell that pesticide to all sorts," she said.

"But not to anyone else connected with St James's," responded Fred. "The police asked me for a list, but I realized I hadn't put ACORN on it. It was very informal. But now it'll look like I… well, like they've… got something to hide."

A thick fall of wisteria behind them shook, making her start. A pigeon flapped away in flurry of wings.

"Should I mention it, do you think?" Fred's eyes widened with childlike trust. "To the police, I mean."

She watched the pigeon fly up into a tree across the Close. She knew she wasn't responsible for Trevor Shoesmith's suicide, but her repeating of that piece of gossip to Ben had had consequences. If she had held her tongue, perhaps she might have had the opportunity to visit the farmer. He would have been her new neighbour, after all. She liked to think that she would have realized just how deep Trevor Shoesmith's desperation ran. She imagined herself sitting talking to him in his kitchen, helping him… but she was fantasizing. The daydream shattered. There was no changing the past, but she could be more responsible in her actions this time. If she told Fred to keep the information to himself, then Ben would call that withholding evidence, and he'd have a pretty good point.

"I think," she began slowly, "you should let them know." She straightened up, speaking more decisively. "Yes, tell them, and be honest about your oversight. I'd like to go and see this farm. Have a bit of a nose around."

Fred liked her plan. He even offered to introduce her to the diocesan agent, Luke McIvor. "He'll be at the funeral, Friday," he said. He shook his big head sadly. "Poor Trevor. He was a lonely man,".

"Did you know him well?"

"Oh no! I knew him by sight, of course, but he kept himself to himself. We'd nod – you know," Fred illustrated his words with the reserved nod of the English country acquaintance, "if we passed in the lane. I walk the dog there – in that lane by his farm. I keep him in the car. He likes it better than being left alone at home."

Faith's comprehension lagged a step behind. He was talking of his dog. She imagined him with a cocker spaniel or maybe a terrier. It struck her how little she knew of Fred. They sat here talking like old friends, and yet she had never asked about the details of his life.

"So you're not married, then?" she enquired.

"Widowed." Fred took a breath as if gathering himself up. "My Joan passed away five years ago this August," he said poignantly. He almost seemed to shrink a little.

"I am so sorry for your loss," she said.

"Thank you. It near broke my heart to lose her." He rallied. "But there's my sister lives just over the way. Five nieces and a nephew," he said with pride. "Joan and I weren't blessed, but I am a fortunate man."

"Mr Partridge, oh, Mr Partridge!" the voice was coy and coquettishly feminine. A sixty-something woman, with trailing clothes and improbably yellow hair, approached them down the path. Fred stood up, and Faith copied him. He looked faintly guilty as he stepped away from her side.

"Mrs May."

"There you are!" Mrs May sized Faith up with a sidelong glance. She didn't seem to like making eye contact with strangers. Whenever her gaze wandered in the direction of Faith's face, her eyes squeezed shut. "I've been looking all over. They said you'd arrived, but no sign of you."

"Faith, Miss Morgan, may I introduce Mrs Tilda May, one of our leading ladies – from St Peter's, down the road."

Mrs May was looking at their feet. It would seem she regarded Faith's presence as an intrusion. Faith had the unworthy desire to slip her hand under Fred's arm, just to see her reaction.

Fred was chattering. "The bishop has arranged for the Reverend Morgan to support us at St James's you see," he was saying. "We're very blessed. Very grateful."

Mrs May interposed herself between them. To Faith's amusement, she linked her arm in Fred's and steered him away.

"Now, Fred, you know I was hoping to have a word with you about the Christian Aid fund-raiser next month, and now there's hardly ten minutes before the meeting starts." She flicked Faith a lightning look, a false smile contorting her face. "So pleased to have met you."

Faith watched them go. Bother! She'd meant to talk to Fred about her idea for a church cleansing ceremony – she'd have to catch him later. If Mrs May would let her…

There were some thirty people gathered for the meeting – mostly clergy, and some laity. Faith found herself a chair at the back with a good view of the company. Mrs May adhered firmly to Fred, and she preferred her solitude.

The deanery incorporated both town and country parishes. The younger family men from the suburban parishes had a busy greyhound look, contrasting with the rural clergy from the villages, older men in traditional black and a sprinkling of tough, motherly-looking women in sensible shoes. Faith felt a bit overdressed. Fashion didn't seem to have penetrated the deanery. At least there was more variety about the gathering than there would have been ten years ago, she reflected. Several of the clergy wore their dog collars with casual dress like jeans or cords, and every now and then coloured clerical shirts broke the monotony of the traditional black or grey. One jolly deaconess was sporting a clerical blouse in racing green. Faith wondered where she had got it. Probably a website – the Americans were far more adventurous than the English.

The rural dean called the meeting to order. After referring briefly and euphemistically to the "troubles" at St James's, and urging members to keep the parishioners in their prayers, he went on to pay tribute to Alistair Ingram and the many years of good service he had brought to his flock. Faith found that several pairs of eyes naturally drifted towards her, and she nodded in gratitude as the rural dean concluded his eulogy.

For the next couple of hours, Faith applied herself to following the agenda of budgets, parish quotas, mission statements, and opportunities for continuing education. A discussion of a Mothers' Union paper on prostitution grew quite heated. One of the laity, a plump, middle-aged man with round red cheeks and a businessman's blue striped suit, was on the point of storming out when the rural dean skilfully brought the meeting to a close, and everyone left their chairs to gather around the tea urns.

"So, how do you find us?" asked her neighbour, a neat-featured clergyman with gold wire-rimmed spectacles. He was dressed in full high-church black. "Neil Steppins – St Jude's. And you're the new girl – Faith Morgan, parachuted in all the way from Birmingham to help out the stricken folk of St James's." He pursed his lips and twinkled at her slyly.

"How do you do?" She shook hands. His nails were beautifully manicured.

"So, not too dull?" he chirped.

"Not all. That last discussion was rather lively," Faith answered, watching the irate businessman who had been cornered by the jolly deaconess, with a cup of coffee and a biscuit.

"Mr Prudhoe?" Neil followed her gaze. "Oh, he's always working himself up into a lather about something. It's traditional at these affairs. Highlight of my morning. But tell me the gossip. *What* about Alistair Ingram!"

His delivery was amusing, but Faith wasn't certain what to make of his frank curiosity. She smiled and didn't respond.

"A murder at Little Worthy. I suppose it looks the part." He nibbled the edge of a ginger nut, his eyes wandering over the company. "Village green, cottages and flowery gardens – that Miss Marple look." He sighed, glancing at her sideways. "Poor Alistair. Murdered. Who knows, maybe Mammon caught up with him."

What did he mean? She wouldn't have cast Neil Steppins as a Puritan.

"Because he used to be a money man in the City? That's a bit severe."

"Oh! Not that! We all like a bit of money – don't we – if we're honest? No. I heard he'd left the City under a cloud all those moons ago. One might think it all forgotten, but when something like this happens…" He brought his cup to his lips. "One does wonder." He sipped his coffee.

What's his game? Faith wondered. Neil was eyeing her quizzically, waiting for her to lob his conversational tennis ball back.

"What happened?" she asked, slightly annoyed that her curiosity had been piqued by what was likely hearsay, and at worse, scurrilous gossip.

"The partnership Alistair worked for got caught out in embezzlement or fraud or something; one of those cases where the investors lost everything."

"And Ingram was prosecuted?"

"Not that I heard, but I seem to remember his partners were."

"That sounds as if he wasn't involved." The impression was forming that Neil Steppins got pleasure out of stirring things up.

"Ah! But perhaps some irate investor might have thought he was." Mr Steppins looked thoughtful. "I wonder if the police know."

"Perhaps you should tell them," Faith said curtly.

"Me? Oh no! I don't know anything really." He shrugged off the responsibility. "Can't even remember who told me, it's all so long ago now – but I'm sure they could check."

Through the crowd Faith saw Canon Matthews heading for the door.

"Excuse me. I must catch a word with the rural dean," she said and left him.

Canon Matthews was an old warhorse of a clergyman. For an older man with unruly grey hair, he moved at quite a pace. Faith followed as he headed for the cloisters, his mobile phone to his ear. He finished his call. She caught up with him just as he scribbled a note in his diary.

"Canon Matthews – I am sorry to disturb you but I wondered if you expected Bishop Anthony this morning? I was told he might be dropping by."

"Miss Morgan – Faith. Yes, the bishop. Bishop Anthony has been called away on a family matter. I am sure if you have a word with Margaret, his secretary, she'll make you an appointment." He seemed to catch up with himself and added: "Actually, there is something I need to speak with you about. How are you managing at St James's?"

"I'm keeping my head above water – I think."

They began to stroll together side by side beneath the colonnade. The canon seemed to find it hard to stand still, as if his legs needed to keep pace with his brain.

"You'll keep an eye on young Donald, will you?" He looked down at her over his spectacles. "Blackney's handling the funeral arrangements – he's an old friend of mine, and his family has been in the business for generations."

Faith felt a little breathless. "Yes, about that," she said, realizing she might not get another chance. "I'm not sure how Don will feel: he's not really all that fond of—"

Canon Matthews sucked a sharp breath through his teeth. "Ah yes! The poor lad thought he could have a private affair, but it won't do. Not in these circumstances. George Casey will handle the press – that's a blessing. The media lads and lasses need someone to keep them in line. We won't let them film in the church, but we can't shut them out entirely. There'll have to be some stand-ups outside the church." The jargon sounded odd from his lips, but he displayed a faint pleasure in his knowledge of the term. "Are you game? It does us good to give a young female face to the church. George tells me we old chaps just look too stuffy."

"But has Don Ingram agreed to all this?" Faith suspected that there was no stopping things now, but she wanted to raise a small flag for the son's rights.

Canon Matthews looked faintly puzzled.

"I phoned him last night. Actually, that's what I had to speak with you about. Donald asked if you wouldn't mind taking part in the service."

"He did?" She felt her cheeks flush pink with surprise and pleasure.

"I've drawn up an order of service," Canon Matthews was saying. "I've put you down for some prayers. I'll email you a copy," he went on. "Let's make a date for a phone consultation, and we can go through it."

In the rural dean's diary she glimpsed a dense mass of times, arrows, and notes in a tiny, spidery hand. It made her ashamed of the remaining white spaces in hers. They reached the end of the colonnade and turned back in silence.

"You found that farmer, Shoesmith, I hear," Canon Matthews said abruptly, as they approached the path. "How are you coping?"

Faith paused. His face was very kind. It seemed important to be honest.

"I am struggling a little, I suppose." Her smile felt tight. "Trevor Shoesmith's life was such a tragedy. It's the old dilemma. How can a loving God permit such misery?"

Canon Matthews nodded his grey head.

"And no one tried to help him?"

She thought of Jessica. "Someone did. But for all their good intentions – maybe they made it worse."

And my loose words may have helped push him over the edge. The thought stung.

"A light in the darkness." The phrase caught her attention.

"A light in the darkness," Canon Matthews repeated, putting a hand on her shoulder. "This is only a moment in time. We Christians are supposed to take the long view. I am aware of your professional background, Faith, of course, but could you be in danger of becoming a little over-involved in the police investigation?"

That was the question, but nevertheless Faith felt a little spurt of annoyance hearing it expressed out loud like that. In the distance, a cluster of clergymen in traditional black suits were walking slowly towards them, deep in discussion. She stared in their direction.

"I suppose I am finding it a little hard to distinguish the boundaries of my role." She looked at up at the grey-haired man beside her. "Aren't we supposed to do all we can to pursue the truth?"

"We're supposed to uphold the truth…" Canon Matthews corrected her – a little patronizingly, she thought.

"But what if you aren't sure what the truth is?"

Canon Matthews fixed her over his spectacles. "As ministers of the gospel, we're not here to pursue the truth," he said.

"We're not?" Faith was shocked. There was a twinkle in his eye. He must have a point.

"Or should I say, the *secular* truth. Our job," he clarified, "is to proclaim the Good News of Christ. For the rest..." his voice took on a rich pulpit note, "Render unto Caesar the things that are Caesar's." He gathered himself up. "I must go. I have a meeting. If young Donald has any questions, get him to give me a ring – any time. Until our next!" He waved a hand cheerily above his head as he loped off in the direction of Church House. He was barely a few yards down the path before he was intercepted by the approaching vicars, and drawn into their discussion.

Render unto Caesar. Not exactly helpful. Which bits were Caesar's?

It would be helpful if God could be more precise in his communications, Faith thought crossly, and headed back in the direction of her car.

CHAPTER

13

GEORGE CASEY STOOD OUTSIDE CHURCH HOUSE talking
to a small group of casually dressed men and women by the car
imprinted with the TV station's logo. Faith's stomach rumbled.
She did a quick about-turn and headed for the high street in
search of somewhere to eat.

The first place was a chain outlet. It had no spaces left –
except for one of those uncomfortably high bar stools, and those
gave her indigestion. She spied a small independent café with a
homely look, and crossed the street.

She opened the half-glass door. A steamy warmth redolent of
sausages in onion gravy enveloped her. She entered just in time to
see the last free table grabbed by a couple of shoppers overflowing
with bags. She scanned the room. Alison, Bishop Anthony's wife,
was sitting alone at a table in the far corner by the window, lost in
thought. Should she go over? It would be an intrusion.

"*Excuse* me!" said a man in a suede jacket impatiently, as
he reached beyond her for some condiments set out on a table
against the wall. She stepped to one side and Mrs Beech saw her.
The bishop's wife looked around, noting the crowded tables.

"Faith!" she called out. "Come sit here with me. I've just been
having a coffee." She brushed up some crumbs from the table and
absent-mindedly deposited them in her coffee cup. There were
grey smudges under her eyes.

"I've just come from my first deanery meeting," Faith said, balancing her umbrella against the window and taking off her coat.

Mrs Beech smiled, but Faith could see that her eyes wanted to wander off into the middle distance.

"What can I get you?" asked the waitress.

Faith resisted the temptation of the sausages and settled for carrot and coriander soup.

"I was hoping to have a word with Bishop Anthony," Faith said, as she watched the waitress retreat. "I understand he's been called away... I hope everything is all right? If you'll excuse my saying, you look worried."

Mrs Beech's eyes focused on her. "Yes." She fiddled with her cup. "I am worried," she said with emphasis. "We've had some worrying news from Tanzania."

"Where your son lives?"

"We're glad he's home, but it's our daughter-in-law. Celia's a health worker with Care United. She's been working with refugees from the conflicts in Burundi and the Congo at a big refugee camp on the border. There's always tension between the camp and the locals, but a friend of Anthony's rang us today to say it's getting very unsettled; there've been riots."

Faith made a sympathetic noise. "And you're worried about Celia?"

"We haven't had an email from her for ten days. We can't seem to raise her – but phone lines do tend to be a problem, particularly at times of trouble."

"Your son must be beside himself."

"Simon's very worried. We all are. He's been trying to get a flight back, but there's nothing at the moment. He and Anthony have spent the morning phoning. Simon has a contact at the embassy in Dodoma. Apparently the area's been sealed off – even embassy staff are having trouble getting in."

"It must be terrible," Faith said.

"We have to wait for the people on the ground to get back to us," said Alison. "Simon's gone down to Blossom Cottage – our retirement cottage," Alison continued in response to the query on Faith's face. "In Lymington. We bought it years back while we were still in Africa."

The waitress arrived with Faith's soup and a warm, crusty roll. It was home-made, fragrant and tasty.

"We're all very fond of the cottage," Alison said, watching Faith eat. "It's the most peaceful place, just by the golf course. Lots of open space."

"It must be very hard for your son, and so worrying for you all," Faith said, mentally kicking herself for sounding so inane. She wondered if she should change the subject.

Mrs Beech looked out into the street.

"I've been worried for some time," she said, her voice distant.

Faith had the impression she was listening in on private thoughts. She kept very still.

"Celia's not one to complain," the older woman went on, "but reading between the lines…" Her pale eyes met Faith's. Careworn, Faith thought; that's the expression. She looks careworn. "Simon has to travel quite a distance to reach his work. Some weeks they hardly see one another, and of course WATA's financial problems have been a strain," Alison began, and then stopped.

"Every couple goes through a sticky patch or two." Faith found herself talking to fill the gap. "And when you are working far from home, that must add to the pressures." What platitudes! I'm not being much help here, she thought, sipping her soup. What wisdom could she possibly offer a woman who had probably been married nearly forty years?

The same thought must have occurred to Alison.

"Yes, of course," she agreed, with something of her old briskness.

Faith used a piece of roll to mop up the last traces in her bowl. As she popped it in her mouth, Alison leaned towards her across the table.

"May I ask? You are single yourself?"

Faith swallowed, taken aback by the switch in direction. Alison's light eyes were fixed on her face with an intensity that was quite disconcerting.

"Ah, yes…"

"But you've had what the young people call 'relationships'?"

Faith wasn't sure she wanted to discuss her personal life with the bishop's wife – but given the present confessional atmosphere, she didn't see how she could avoid the question.

"Before I came into the church," Faith replied, picking her words carefully, "I did live with a man for several years."

"And it was a committed relationship?"

Faith thought of how deeply she had been in love with Ben in those days. She had imagined they would spend their lives together.

"Yes."

"So why didn't you marry?" Alison asked. The question might have been accusatory, but the bishop's wife merely sounded intrigued.

Faith stared at her for a moment. This was getting close to the bone.

"When the question finally came up, I found I wasn't sure that we were compatible."

"And yet you lived together for years?"

"Some three years."

"It took you so long to discover this… incompatibility?"

"We encountered extraordinary circumstances."

"And he didn't pass the test?"

The bishop's wife's simple question stung. Faith had never looked at it that way before. She didn't know what to say. Mrs Beech's sincerity seemed to cut right through all her defences, leaving her vulnerable and uncertain.

Alison reached out and covered her hand as it lay beside her empty bowl.

"Human beings do fail, you know; sometimes they stumble,

sometimes they can go quite awry. But that is what love is about. Real love grows out of failures and forgiveness as much as a mutual passion. It is something that takes two people a lifetime to learn."

She fell silent. All around them, shoppers gossiped and drank and ate. Faith waited.

"But there can be some very hard times," said Alison sadly, her eyes fixed on the middle distance. She straightened her shoulders. "Was there something you wanted to speak to the bishop about?" she said in her old manner. It seemed that the confessional part of the conversation was over.

"It's not important."

Alison went on as if Faith hadn't spoken. "I've sent Anthony up to the farm. It always cheers him up to have a walk around. You can catch him there."

"I wouldn't want to disturb him – he's been having such a day..."

"Nonsense. It is simple to find ACORN, you just take the Andover road towards Itchen Abbas." Mrs Beech took a pencil out of her handbag and drew directions on a napkin. "It'll do him good to have something else to think about. If you go now you should still catch him."

It seemed she was being dismissed. Faith got out her purse and counted out payment for her bill.

"If there is anything I can do to help, you will let me know?" She knew the offer was practically pointless, but it seemed important to make it.

"You can keep Celia in your prayers."

"Of course." Faith picked up the little map of directions to ACORN. She said her goodbyes and left.

It was an idyllic piece of country on the banks of the River Itchen. Faith spotted an open gate, marked with a simple drawing of an acorn, leading down a track – old established woods to one side, and pasture on the other. The recent rain had buffed up the vivid green. A herd of black-faced ewes and their lambs were grazing at the scrubby grass. Faith rolled down her window and breathed in the fresh air. Well, she'd wanted to check out the ACORN farm, and now here she was. Her car bumped across a cattle grid. The track sloped downwards and turned a corner. A group of silvery wooden barns with traditional red-tiled roofs appeared facing one another around a large sandy square.

She drew up in a parking space alongside a minivan with "ACORN Produce" stencilled on the side. Across the way, a group of black and white saddleback pigs with large, floppy ears were rooting around in a pen. One poked its head through the fence, resting its chin on the bar as it contemplated her. It looked cheerful. She went over and scratched its bristly head between its ears.

"So where is everyone?" she asked. "Have you seen a passing bishop, by any chance?"

The pig shifted its weight and sighed. She spotted a sign, "Farm Shop", high up on a barn wall. A board hung beneath it: "Open" it read, with an arrow below pointing across the square.

If it's open, there should be someone there, she thought.

She had crossed the square wondering whether to go left or right, when she spotted a couple in the middle distance walking towards her. Two men – and one of them was Ben.

She thought of the abrupt end to their last conversation. Just her luck to run into Ben now. She resisted the temptation to turn back. Taking a deep breath, she walked on at a steady pace, controlling the urge to speed up.

The gap between them closed as if in slow motion. It was hard work keeping a pleasant half-smile on her face, but she'd rather that than pretend to look at something out of their eye-line. Ben was talking. His companion contemplated her with frank curiosity. A stocky young man with thick black hair and rosy cheeks wearing a Barbour jacket and red corduroy trousers, he didn't quite fit her idea of an ACORN person – his Barbour was too new and his trousers too red. Ben made some remark.

The other man laughed. Ben wore his sardonic look.

Just three yards to go…

"Church meeting over for the day?" Ben greeted her sarcastically.

"I'm looking for Bishop Anthony – someone said I might find him here," she responded, transferring her attention to his companion. She held out her hand.

"Hello. I'm Faith Morgan. I am helping out at St James's Church in Little Worthy for the interim."

"Of course! Luke McIvor, diocesan agent. Bishop Beech has mentioned you." He pumped her hand a little overenthusiastically. So this was the man she'd heard so much about. His voice had an Irish lilt. "Sorry to say you've just missed the bishop. He left ten minutes ago."

Faith felt a twinge of frustration. Not only was it a wasted trip, but with Ben looking over her shoulder, she might not even get an opportunity to ask McIvor about the mystery at St James's.

McIvor registered her disappointment. His expression was cheerful, although Faith thought she detected just a touch of mischief.

"But don't you be rushing off. I'm just giving Inspector Shorter the tour. Join us, why don't you?"

Out of the corner of her eye, Faith caught the flash of annoyance on Ben's face.

"I would love to," she responded, matching McIvor's enthusiasm. She fell in beside him. "Bishop Anthony has told me such good things about this project. Tell me, who runs ACORN?" she asked chattily.

"There's a wide group of supporters and some volunteers, but the management team comes down to three: Sandy and George – they're a couple – and their partner, Bill."

They both seemed to be ignoring Ben, who marched on the far side of the agent, his gaze fixed straight ahead.

"And are they about?"

"Not this afternoon – they're attending a farmers' market

meeting in Andover – so you're stuck with me, sad to say."

He smiled broadly at her, and she grinned back.

"You were going to show me the stores…" Ben cut in impatiently.

"Of course! This way." Luke McIvor twinkled at Faith. He didn't seem in awe of Ben at all. She liked him immediately.

"The inspector's checking me out as a purveyor of poisons," he said. "That'll teach me to buy pesticides."

Faith was puzzled. "You buy them on ACORN's behalf?" she asked.

"Not exactly. As I was explaining to the inspector, this is an organic farm, as is the neighbouring farm, but we've been having a bit of a pest problem of late. The neighbouring farmer says it's lax control by ACORN, and has insisted on a treated buffer zone between his land and ACORN's. As agent for their diocesan landlords, I'm playing mediator."

"But ACORN aren't keen?" Faith suggested.

Luke McIvor gave the laugh of a man who bore no grudges. "They stockpile the stuff I give them and tell me they'll get on to it. They never have yet. I understand why; the other farmer's got fifty times as much land – they want him to sacrifice some of that for the buffer."

He stopped before a padlocked shed. He brought out a key and unlocked it. "There." He pointed to a pile of cans bearing the brand logo of a leading chemical company. "That's all I've purchased from Partridge's Feed and Supply."

Ben went over and picked up one can, and then another. He shook it. Liquid sloshed audibly inside.

"This one's been used," he said.

"Couple of weeks back, I siphoned off a pint for Mrs Beech, the bishop's wife," Luke explained. "She was telling me of an aphid problem with her roses. I told her a bit of that, fifty-fifty diluted with water, sprayed on them of an evening, that'll put paid to them."

Now, what was Ben going to make of that? Faith shot a look

at him, and saw his eyebrows lift a fraction. Even he couldn't suspect the bishop's wife did it.

They filed out of the shed. Ben waited for Faith to go first, half blocking the doorway.

"Who has keys?" Ben's voice splashed like a stone into their easy conversation.

Luke pulled the door closed and threaded the padlock through the hasp.

"To this place? I've got this one," he patted his pocket, "and then there's George's – he carries a big bunch of keys around with him at all times." He relocked the padlock and gave it a tug. "I think he sleeps with the darned things. And I believe there's a spare in the office safe."

Ben looked unconvinced.

"We keep a careful check on these stocks," Luke said defensively. He seemed to think Ben was impugning his professionalism. "George and Sandy don't even like to have the stuff on the property. They don't want it getting about that they use it. All I bought is still there – minus that pint; I can show you the invoices if you'd like."

Ben grunted.

Luke led them up to a vantage point looking down on the farm buildings, with the river meandering peacefully beyond.

"There are some fine watercress beds down there," he said, pointing towards the riverbank. "Very popular at the farm shop. Clover-rich, these meadows. Grand for beef cattle."

Even under grey skies it was a charming place. Faith watched a pair of lambs gambolling as if they were posing for a child's picture book.

"Where are the cattle?" she asked. "I don't see them."

Luke grinned at her. "Oh, Sandy takes too good care of them. The spring's been so wet, she's still feeding them inside. I'll take you round that way. They're fine beasts. South Devons, a good old native British breed. Grand meat – very sweet." He gazed about. "I love the land here," he said.

"I presume, then, that the offer you made for the Shoesmith farm was on your own behalf?"

Faith stared at Ben. She only just managed to keep her mouth shut. Where had that come from? He lifted an eyebrow at her.

Luke McIvor drew himself up. "Well, now, how did you know about that?" he asked Ben.

"His papers."

"I made Shoesmith an offer to buy his farm, yes." McIvor set off back down the path to the farm. "He clearly hadn't been managing for months – years, even. You wouldn't know it to look at it now, but that land's good land. The state of it!" His voice betrayed a flash of disgust, then just as swiftly he resumed his easy charm, switching back into tour-guide mode.

"Conservation trails. Open to the public," he said, gesturing to a wooden signpost at the junction of two paths leading into the woods. "ACORN's keen on educating the young. In fact we've just had grand news; a lottery grant's come through for the new education centre."

"Funded by the proceeds of gambling?" Ben said cynically, with a sideways glance at Faith. "I thought the church would have a position on that?"

She ignored him.

"So you made Shoesmith a firm offer?" Ben resumed, slipping back into his track.

"It was no secret."

Faith examined the land agent's face. His expression was open and honest as far as she could judge.

"He wasn't interested." Luke addressed her as if she were an ally. "I think he still had hopes he would have children of his own one day."

Faith thought of Jessica. "Really?"

"Gave me the hint he had the lady all picked out. Hoping to be fruitful and multiply. It was quite a change in him."

"When was this?"

Luke grimaced thoughtfully. "Oh, just around Christmas." He

shrugged. "And now he's dead. I guess she turned him down."

They were approaching a long barn with solar panels on the roof. The sound of cattle lowing came through the open door. Faith glimpsed a large reddish bull with a ring in its nose standing in a stall gazing peacefully at nothing.

"That's Arthur – isn't he a fine fellow?" said Luke automatically. He checked his watch.

Faith saw a neat pile of manure by the door.

"Do you remember an incident when Alistair Ingram found manure dumped in the vicarage drive?" she asked suddenly.

Luke paused. "Indeed I do," he replied. "Back in January, I think."

Faith contemplated the mound. It was bulky stuff. It looked heavy, too – and messy.

"How much was there? Just a bag-full, or…"

"Oh, more than that. As I remember, it took my man more than an hour to shift it away – or at least, that's what he billed me for."

That suggested someone with access to farm equipment.

"So whoever dumped it had a trailer or some such?" she pondered out loud. Ben watched her with a flicker of amusement in his eyes.

"Do you think Trevor Shoesmith did it?" she asked Luke. "I understand he had a dispute with the vicar of St James's over some land issue?"

"The Shoesmith family have been in dispute with St James's over a covenanted field for generations," Luke agreed. "Yes. I did think Trevor might have been responsible – although I wouldn't have said it was his sort of behaviour. But Ingram certainly blamed Shoesmith at first – then he changed his mind. Quite odd."

"What happened?" asked Ben.

"I honestly don't know." Luke shrugged. "The morning he found the stuff, Alistair was straight on the phone to me, all fired up and complaining. Then a couple of hours later, he sends me an email saying he'd rethought his position and decided it would be best to ignore the whole thing. Didn't want me to say any more about it. I phoned back, but he was adamant. So I sent a man over; he shovelled it all up and Ingram's garden got a good feed. His bulbs were looking grand this spring."

Why should Ingram suddenly change his mind? Christian charity? Did he find something out in those two hours? Faith realized that she was looking at Ben and he at her. She was almost certain they had the same thoughts: Blackmail? Or maybe a warning?

But by whom, and what was at stake?

CHAPTER

14

A BRISK BREEZE MOVED THE FLOWERS in the gardens around Little Worthy green. With luck, the weather might hold for the funeral tomorrow. As she opened the vestry door, Faith braced herself. Why should she have assumed that anyone would be free to turn out at such short notice for a church cleansing at ten o'clock on a Thursday morning? She couldn't have been thinking straight. Never mind. If just Fred turned up, they would make a go of it together.

She heard voices from the body of the church beyond the vestry. A well-rounded lady in a 1950s-style pinafore apron came into view, mopping the tiles. She turned and smiled.

"Vicar Faith!" The lady with the soft silver hair pinned up in a bun who she had seen with Pat on her first day bobbed up from behind a pew, a bright yellow duster in hand.

"Elsie Lively," she said in a soft, breathy voice, "… seen me at church…"

"Indeed I do remember you," Faith responded warmly. "And from before that. You used to have the post office. I remember your jars with those jewel-like boiled sweets; they were so pretty."

Elsie looked pleased. "My sister, Grace…" She turned to the lady with the mop. Grace was her sister's plumper copy – apart from the fact that she wore her hair short and permed.

Fred bustled up from the back of the church with three other members of the congregation. Faith recognized two of them from the Sunday before – the black man who had phoned for the ambulance, and his wife. Fred introduced them properly as Timothy and Clarisse Johnston. Timothy was a big, calm presence of a man. His wife came up to his shoulder. She was slim and elegant and wore a vivid African scarf bound round her head, turban-fashion. With them was their friend Sue, a buxom young mother with lively dark eyes and a rich chuckle.

"My fellow churchwarden sends her apologies," said Fred cheerily. "There's a Mothers' Union committee meeting at the cathedral this morning and Pat never misses those."

"I am so pleased to see you all," said Faith.

"I think this is a lovely idea," said Grace. "Very moving," she murmured, and resumed mopping the tiles. Elsie sighed sympathetically and returned to polishing the pew.

"We're working back from the chancel," said Sue, holding out a cloth to Faith. "Duster?"

For the best part of half an hour, the small group polished and dusted in silence, cleaning the pews and the candlesticks, the window ledges, and the choir stalls. Faith gave the lectern a good polish and laid down a freshly laundered altar cloth. Fred went round with a brush, while Elsie and Grace wiped the glass of the noticeboards and restocked the leaflets, before making sure the prayer books were neatly aligned. Shafts of sunlight caught the rising swirls of dust.

"So tell me about Alistair Ingram," said Faith, as she replaced a candle in its sconce.

"I liked him," said Sue.

"He was a good man," agreed Clarisse.

"We all liked him." Timothy's voice was a rich baritone. Faith almost fancied she could feel the air vibrate as he spoke. "He was a good pastor; his sermons had substance."

Sue straightened up, holding an old-fashioned two-pronged hairpin between finger and thumb. "Elsie!" she called out. "I've found one of your pins!"

There was a muffled response from Elsie, who was occupied in the vestry.

"I'll give it to her later," said Sue, pocketing the pin.

Faith found the labour comforting, even though her knees suffered on the stone flags. Having completed the main body of the church, the seven of them stood in silence in front of the altar where Alistair died – a spot Faith realized they'd all been avoiding. Timothy picked up a bucket of steaming water that was standing by the steps.

"We are here to clean, are we not?" He walked calmly behind the altar. He folded his large frame to kneel down where Alistair Ingram had fallen, and began to wash the tiles. Faith picked up a cloth and joined him. Sue and Clarisse set to work on the altar rail, and Fred tackled the wooden panelling under the windows.

We are going to be all right, Faith thought.

Just after eleven o'clock, she stood up to stretch her back.

"A job well done," she said. "Thank you, everyone. We should say a prayer."

They all nodded, and Faith bowed her head before the altar – not the leader of a congregation today, but one of them. The ceremony tomorrow would bring with it the full solemnity of the church and its authority, and at least some of the words she spoke then would follow the practiced patterns of established grieving.

Now she spoke informally of farewells, and remembrance, and having strength as a community to overcome difficult times. When she finished, and the "Amens" echoed around the circle, she looked up to see all six were smiling at her. "Thank you," Faith repeated.

As the group broke, Sue looked at her watch. "Dave will be opening the Hare and Hounds," she said. "I could murder an orange and lemonade."

The suggestion brought mumbles of approval from the others, including Faith.

"I think we all deserve it," she said. She looked at the

light-flooded nave, her nose twitching at the lingering scent of disinfectant. They could never erase what had happened, but they could start afresh. For the first time since setting foot in St James's, she felt a sense of belonging.

Having cleared away the cloths and emptied the buckets down the drain outside, they said goodbye to Grace and Elsie.

"We'll be back to help Pat with the flowers after lunch," said Grace, as she and Elsie put on their coats.

The remaining five trooped across the green to the pub. Faith treated her parishioners to a round of drinks, and they sat at a table outside. Despite the sunshine, the infrequent breeze brought Faith's arms out in goose pimples.

"Has anyone seen Jessica?" she asked.

All four pairs of eyes turned to her as one.

"I don't think she would have been able to handle it," said Sue. An uncomfortable silence fell, until she added, "You knew, of course, about Alistair and Mrs Rose?"

Now everyone seemed to be looking into their drinks. Fred's meaty fingers ran up and down his glass of bitter shandy.

"I did," said Faith carefully, "though I had no idea it was common knowledge."

"Oh, yes," Clarisse said. "They were discreet, but I think it was obvious they cared for one another."

Faith smiled. She should have known there couldn't be secrets in a place like Little Worthy. "And no one objected?"

"Why should they? It was nobody's business but their own." Sue was emphatic.

"I thought they were well suited," offered Timothy. "They both deserved a bit of loving companionship after what they'd been through."

Faith pricked up her ears. "Jessica had suffered too?"

"A messy divorce." Sue pulled a sympathetic face. "Poor Jessica. She married a rat. He walked out on her one Christmas Eve."

"He'd been having an affair with a woman at work for over

two years, and she had no idea," explained Clarisse. "Jessica believes in the sanctity of marriage – she trusted him."

"I heard he was a deacon in his church," added Timothy.

"Not in a proper church," responded Sue dismissively. "One of those Praise and Glory sects. Hypocrite."

Faith thought Fred looked like he'd rather be anywhere else. Gossip obviously wasn't his thing, poor chap.

"How about Pat?" Faith asked. "Did she know about them – Alistair and Jessica, I mean?"

She glanced at her companions. She wondered how open they would be with her. She was, after all, the outsider. Pat was one of them. She had already formed the impression that Pat Montesque disapproved of the "blonde divorcee", as Don had described Jessica – but how far did it go?

"I'm not sure about Pat," said Clarisse slowly. "Did she know?" she asked Sue.

Sue wrinkled her nose. "Probably, but I don't think she wanted to recognize publicly that she knew – if you know what I mean. Pat does so believe in keeping up appearances." Sue leaned forward over her glass. "With Pat I think it's more that she had to put up with her unsatisfactory husband, so why should anyone else get a break!"

Faith almost choked on her drink. "Pat has a husband?" She immediately wished she hadn't sounded so surprised. Timothy was grinning now.

"Not any more," said Sue. "Gordon – he was still alive when Jerry and I first moved here. You'd have been here a year or so, wouldn't you, Clari?" Clarisse nodded.

"He wasn't sociable like Pat," said Sue briskly. "A bit of a grump."

"He was an invalid," Clarisse reminded her.

Sue shrugged. "Very Scottish – dour."

"Pat always looked after him beautifully," stated Clarisse.

"Her calling," said Sue. Clarisse grimaced good-humouredly. "You've got to admit, she was glad to free be of him," Sue insisted.

"She blossomed when he died."

"What did her husband do for a living?" Faith knew she was being nosey, but she wondered how Pat had ended up with her expensive house on the green.

Sue frowned thoughtfully. "I *think* he inherited a business from his family and sold it. Didn't do anything when I knew him. As Clari says, he was an invalid," she said, making air quotes around the word. Sue clearly didn't think much of Pat's dear departed. "He left Pat in a precarious situation after he died. Bad investments. She nearly lost the house."

"Poor thing!" exclaimed Faith, and hoped she didn't sound insincere. "When was that?"

"Oh, a few years ago. Before Alistair Ingram's time. But she got back on her feet – nothing keeps 'La Montesque' down for long. Everything seems to be all right now." Sue pulled her coat more tightly around her shoulders. "It's not warm, is it?"

Finances. Faith thought of the wealth that gleamed out from the decorations in Alistair Ingram's vicarage. Despite the cleansing, the grubbiness of the crime still stained her thoughts. Could money be at the bottom of all this?

"I heard that there might have been some financial scandal in Alistair Ingram's past," she said, "before he came into the priesthood?"

Clarisse and Sue looked at each other, their expressions wary. Had she gone too far?

"I was on the lay panel that interviewed Alistair when he first arrived," said Timothy, speaking up for the first time. "He mentioned that business to me when we first met. It was one of the factors that persuaded him that he needed a change of direction. It happened while his wife was dying; a partnership he was associated with as a consultant defrauded several of their investors."

"I don't think Alistair himself was involved," said Fred.

"I believe he was appalled when he found out what had been going on," Timothy added, giving weight to his words as if he were pronouncing them in court. "It was my impression that he blamed himself for not picking up the signs. But he was trying to care for his wife at home and raise their son and those were dark days." He glanced down. "How can you do more than survive through a tragedy like that? Alistair Ingram wasn't to blame. He happened to be deceived by bad men."

A sombre mood descended over the table. Sue drained her glass.

"But they didn't make it obvious by any means," she said, changing the subject back to Jessica. "If you'd gone by appearances, you'd have been more likely to suspect he was having an affair with Pat."

Clarisse gave a little giggle and suppressed it. "Now, Sue!"

"Well, you would. All his cocktail-hour visits to her little cottage!" Sue spoke in a comic parody of the worst kind of gossip. Faith assumed the "little" was sarcasm. Pat's house was one of the best on the green. Fred was squirming, seemingly taking great interest in the pot plants outside the pub.

"Shame on you, woman!" Clarisse's protest was good-natured.

"You're not telling me it was all churchwarden business," responded Sue, still in character. Then she stopped suddenly. "Oh dear," her voice wobbled. "I can't believe I said that." Her cheeks flushed.

Faith put a hand on her arm. "There's no shame in good humour," she said warmly. "It's a proper expression of life. Sin shall not have dominion over us – remember?"

Timothy was contemplating her steadily. "You're looking for motive," he said.

They were all staring at her now. Faith felt a sudden flicker of panic. She didn't want to lose their trust. St James's was beginning to feel like home.

"You are helping the police with their enquiries?" There was humour in Timothy's voice but also steel. Did he disapprove?

If she was to have a future at Little Worthy she would have

to be honest with them.

"I should have said something before," she admitted. "I know the detective inspector in charge of the case. Before I joined the church I was in the police force."

"But how interesting!" exclaimed Clarisse.

"Not the killingly handsome one – tall, dark hair, blue eyes?" demanded Sue. "You lucky beggar! Will you introduce me? On second thoughts, don't." She pulled a face. "The ones that look that good are always a disappointment."

"You already have a husband, you shameless woman!" Timothy boomed.

"I know, I know – and I love him dearly, but I can dream of beefcake, can't I?" responded Sue cheerfully.

Faith felt an unexpected flick of annoyance. Ben was not beefcake.

Now, where had that come from? She pulled her attention back to the present. Fred's mouth was moving and he was looking in her direction.

"… can we help?" he asked. "I'm sure we all want to know who took poor Alistair's life."

Faith cleared her throat.

"Well, I suppose the great question is – did anyone see any strangers about that weekend – or someone who stood out in the weeks before?'

"The police have already asked us this," said Timothy.

"Not me they haven't," said Sue.

"But you weren't here last Sunday," Clarisse responded reasonably.

"True," Sue conceded.

"No one saw any odd strangers about?" insisted Faith.

"We don't get that many strangers in Little Worthy outside the summer months," said Clarisse.

"Pity Pat isn't here," said Sue, quite distinctly. "She's a one-woman neighbourhood watch."

Clarisse laughed. "One time, my cousin – he's a surgeon in

New York – was visiting us, and he arrived after dark in a rental car. Pat had him showing her his passport. He was so intimidated!" She chuckled at the memory.

"Fred regularly walks his dog around the green at odd times; what about you, Fred?" asked Sue. They turned to him.

"I do remember there was a man, a week or so ago. He was sitting in his car at the top of Shoesmith's lane one evening." As Fred spoke, he tapped his hand on the weathered wood of the table. He stopped, realizing he had everyone's attention. "Well, it was probably nothing unusual," he mumbled.

What was the man doing that was so embarrassing? thought Faith, amused. Dear Fred. I hope it was nothing lewd.

"So, what was he up to?" demanded Sue, intrigued.

Fred frowned. "It was none of my business, but it looked as if the poor fellow was crying. I almost went up, but I didn't want to intrude."

"What colour was the car?" asked Faith.

"I'm not sure," Fred pursed his lips. "As I said, it was dusk. I think it would have been a dark colour, though. Not black. Maybe red or blue."

"And you didn't recognize the man?"

Fred shook his head. "Had his face in his hands and I didn't want to stare."

The group, it seemed, had nothing else to offer. They peeled themselves away from the table, and Fred took the glasses back inside.

"What you suggested today," Timothy told Faith, enveloping her hand in the warmth of his, "it was a good thing."

"You must come and have supper with us soon," said Clarisse, hugging her.

"I'm coming, too," Sue added. "I want to hear more about the devastating inspector."

Faith watched them go their separate ways. It is as if they have been visiting me in my home, she thought. How peculiar.

She walked slowly back to the church, and stepped into its cool interior. How could she have assumed Alistair Ingram's place so quickly? Faith felt a sobering wave of guilt. It had only been a few days since she had seen him die here. The poor man's coffin would be borne down this very aisle in less than twenty-four hours.

She heard Canon Matthews's words: *We Christians are supposed to take the long view.*

She stared at the lamb in the glass panel, with its enigmatic and somehow enticing smile.

The truth is there to be revealed. Have hope.

She knelt by the altar rail and prayed. She prayed for Alistair Ingram and for Trevor Shoesmith and the unknown killer. And she felt at peace.

Sometime later she got up. As she turned, a shocked gasp rose in her throat. Jessica was sitting in the fourth pew, watching her.

"Sorry," said Faith. "I didn't hear you come in."

Jessica wore a simple black dress with a scoop neck. The lack of colour drained her face, making it deathly white. Faith went over and sat down beside her. They looked at the altar together in silence.

"I'm sorry I didn't come to the cleaning," said Jessica. "I don't think I could've coped."

"Of course," said Faith.

"I can't believe he's gone." Jessica was so still, Faith had the sense that if she moved she might break. "I know it. I saw it." Jessica frowned. "But I keep catching myself – it's as if my mind flicks the edge of something unimaginable. I know it's there, but I can't look at it. Because if I did…"

The tears welled up. Faith put an arm around her and let her cry. As she waited for the sobs to subside, she remembered a passage in a sermon Canon Jonathan had preached in his church.

It is important to place the hope of the resurrection, the promise of newness and life, against the background of death and endings.

She had never fully appreciated the meaning of that. Jessica's hair was ruffled and dull. She must have forgotten to comb it. Her sobs reverberated through Faith's chest. It was like holding misery incarnate.

It is only in walking through the shadows and darkness of Holy Week and Good Friday. Jonathan's precise voice played in her memory as her eyes focused on the cross above the altar. *It is only by realizing the horror and magnitude of sin and its consequences in the world that we can understand the light and hope of Easter Sunday morning.*

Please God, let there be light after this.

CHAPTER
15

JESSICA TOOK OUT A PACKET OF TISSUES. "Never leave the house without them these days," she said, and blew her nose.

"It's been one hell of week," agreed Faith. That drew a wan smile. Jessica inhaled a long breath and let it out.

"It has."

Bright sunshine illuminated the window behind the altar, touching the cross above it with warmth.

"I hate the person who did this," Jessica said. Her hands clenched in her lap. "I am so *angry*. If I could get my hands on them…"

Faith had a sudden flash of a woman sitting at her kitchen table. Emilia Santa, the mother whose strength and charity when faced with the casual murder of her teenage son had first nudged Faith towards the path that had led her to the ministry. As a young policewoman, she had found Emilia's ability to forgive perplexing and wondrous. Sitting here beside Jessica, she marvelled again. Her own faith seemed paltry in comparison. She, too, was consumed with anger at the poisoner in the shadows. It was all so intangible. No face to blame. No reason for what had happened. What else could one do but rage at the unidentified monster?

"I am supposed to forgive – aren't I?" Jessica appealed to her, her expression intense. "That's what Christians are supposed to do – forgive those who trespass against us? But he's destroyed Alistair, and then Trevor too. I don't believe Trevor would be dead now if all this hadn't happened here. To destroy two good men – that's not trespass, that's evil."

This was where she, Faith Morgan, as a minister of the gospel, ought to offer consolation and wise words. Instead, she felt lost and inadequate. What was the comfort of faith supposed to be in these circumstances?

To weep.

What kind of good news is that! Faith raged internally.

And what is the good news? The words popped up inside her head and sat there.

She was due to preside and preach in this very church on Palm Sunday in a couple of days. She should know the answer to that.

The good news of Christ's death and resurrection is that sin and death do not have the last word; and something about the saving power of God's love, she answered impatiently in her head.

Precisely.

The empty church was peaceful; a contained space with only sunlight penetrating from the outside world.

"My faith has always been important to me." Jessica's voice sounded detached.

"Have you always been a churchgoer?"

Jessica nodded. "My parents were very faithful." Her eyes darted up to Faith's face and then away. "They weren't Church of England – Welsh Baptists."

"Faithful is faithful."

"But after all this…" Jessica moved restlessly on the pew, releasing a waft of fresh polish from the wood.

"You're questioning everything," Faith supplied.

Jessica nodded.

"That's natural. This is all so very recent – all the emotion and shock; you need to give yourself time." Faith paused, casting around for something real to say. "What do you think Alistair would make of it?"

Jessica's mouth twisted in a stubborn look. She shrugged.

"How did you two come to meet?" Faith asked.

Jessica stirred. "Alistair and me?"

"Yes."

"When I moved to Little Worthy my marriage had just broken up. I was divorced – something I never imagined myself being. I needed to… I needed to feel…" she paused and started again. "It was a confusing time. I wanted God to lead me somewhere."

"And he led you here?"

She shrugged again. "Not directly," she said.

Jessica's eyes were fixed on at a spot in the middle distance, a faint frown creasing her forehead.

"I went to go to the cathedral at first. They're used to strangers there. I volunteered for all sorts of projects." Her voice was self-mocking and bitter. "Looking for redemption!"

Faith suspected this savage self-awareness was a new thing to Jessica. She'd seen it before when good people cruising along on unquestioning, simple faith met a terrible crisis. Blind trust in the Lord can prove a brittle thing, Canon Jonathan was fond of saying. The faith that enables you to live with questions is much more robust in the long run.

"But I didn't find what I was looking for." Jessica sat up straighter, stiffening her spine. "Then one day I walked in here – into this church – and I met Alistair. We began to talk. He was such a decent man. He never made you feel small or foolish. When he listened, he made a space where you could just be." She stretched out her hand towards the altar and rested it on the pew back in front of them. "His faith was so open and welcoming. I started coming to St James's – and we would meet around the village. Then we fell in love."

Her lips compressed as she struggled to keep back the tears.

"I keep wondering…" She gave a little sob. "I wonder if this is my punishment?"

Faith was taken aback. "What on earth for?"

"I betrayed God's laws."

What an old-fashioned phrase! Faith stared at the tragic profile of the suffering woman beside her. Could she really believe her divorce would condemn her forever?

"In what way?" she asked cautiously.

Jessica drew herself away into her own space, averting her eyes.

"Before I met Alistair… Oh, how to start!" she exclaimed. "I am so ashamed of this."

"I have done some pretty shameful things in my time," Faith reassured her. "I'm fairly unshockable."

Jessica glanced at her dubiously, but she continued. "I hadn't been long divorced. I was low and lost. I went volunteering on all sorts of charitable projects – as I said. I needed to be less selfish; to get away from myself." Her eyes wandered about the altar in front of them.

"I met a man; a charity worker on one of those projects," Jessica said. "He was so full of purpose…"

Faith had a sudden flash of Ben striding up the path. I understand the attraction of that, she thought.

"So full of his mission." Jessica turned to look at her full face. "The project was abroad, in a foreign country; everything was so very different – the landscape, the colours, the light. I lost my footing."

"How so?"

She dropped her head. "I got involved," she said softly.

So you slept with him? thought Faith impatiently.

"And then I discovered…"

Ah!

"He was married," Faith completed her sentence for her.

"Yes."

Jessica came to life, her voice infused with energy.

"My husband betrayed me like that – away from home with another woman. First I was divorced, and then all of a sudden I was an adulterer. I was never going to be that person." She appealed to Faith. "I was so far from home. Just for an instant, everything seemed perfect. This man – he needed me. He had worked so hard, alone, for so long. He needed someone to work alongside him, to believe in him. He wasn't good with the figures, so I helped him prepare a budget for a meeting with potential sponsors... He was very grateful."

"I know how exciting it can be when you work well together with someone – all the more when there's sexual attraction as well," commented Faith ruefully.

"And he was romantic." Jessica's voice was distant, as if she were looking down on herself from a height. "That night he gave me irises – my favourite flower. They were silk – those imitation ones – but they looked real. We were out in the middle of nowhere. Heaven knows where he got them from."

"And you had no idea he was married?"

"No. It was all fake – just like the flowers." Faith could read the impact of the betrayal on Jessica's face. "And I believed him. When he talked, there was only us. How we'd come back and make our lives together, growing our own food, living in harmony with the land in a cottage by the sea."

That sounded like a teenager's fantasy to Faith.

"I suspect you'd need money in real life," she commented out loud.

A faintly cynical look flashed across Jessica's face. Now she looked all of forty and, to Faith's eyes, even better.

"I can earn plenty enough for two; people always need accountants. When I discovered the truth, I broke it off straight away and came home as soon as I could. I was so ashamed of myself."

"And then you met Alistair."

"Yes. Here." She looked around the church.

"Did you tell him about the affair?"

"Yes." Jessica half-smiled. "The first afternoon we met. I told you he was easy to talk to."

"And what was his verdict?"

"That I'd made a mistake; I'd repented of it, and I should forgive myself." Her face softened. "Alistair taught me a lot about forgiveness."

"It seems he was a good priest."

"He was. And a good man… So you don't think this is my punishment?" she asked in a child's voice.

"Certainly not! My God is a loving God; he is neither petty nor vindictive." Faith was categorical. "And he'd have to be both to sacrifice a good man to punish a simple human mistake. What could possibly be loving about that?"

Jessica didn't look completely convinced, but she seemed a little comforted. She sighed.

"I'm dreading tomorrow," she said quietly. "Trying not to make a fuss in case someone should notice. I don't know how I am going to sit through it, pretending…"

"You don't need to pretend." Jessica's blue eyes swung up to meet Faith's. "People knew what you and Alistair meant to each other – in this church, I mean. You won't be alone, and you don't have to pretend."

As she spoke she made a mental note to ring Fred. If he could pick Jessica up tomorrow, she could take her home herself after the funeral. She glanced at her watch. Nearly two already. Pat and the Lively sisters would be arriving before long to do the funeral flowers. It would be a good idea to get Jessica away before that. She shouldn't have to suffer Pat's scrutiny in her present condition.

"Why don't you go home now and try to get some sleep?" Faith shepherded a docile Jessica to the door. "I'll organize someone to pick you up tomorrow and I'll take you home afterwards myself."

As Jessica was getting into her car, something Clarisse and Sue had talked about earlier surfaced in Faith's mind.

"Jessica – how did Pat get along with Alistair?" she asked. "Were they friends?"

Jessica looked surprised. "Friends? She was his churchwarden, that's all."

"Did the churchwardens have regular meetings with Alistair at Pat's house on the green?"

"No." Jessica leaned back against the headrest wearily. "Alistair wasn't really the type who went round for tea with his parishioners."

"But he would call on Pat to discuss parish business?" insisted Faith. "Is she the parish treasurer? Does she keep the books?"

Jessica frowned as if she was trying to concentrate. "Alistair would call on her in the evening once a week. He was always careful about being on time because Pat would make a fuss if he was late. But Fred's the parish treasurer; he keeps the books."

After she waved Jessica off, Faith checked her emails on her laptop, feeling, as usual, oddly incongruous tapping away at her keyboard in such an ancient setting. The rural dean had been in touch with a broad order of service and some suggestions. Faith made a mental note to discuss some of the finer points with Don, and wondered for the first time if he'd come at all. Crossing the threshold might be too much for him.

Next, she rang the funeral directors, sitting on a bench in the porch to the church. She spoke with Richard Blackney, the current general manager. Soft-spoken and professional, he assured her that everything was prepared, and intimated that the rural dean was handling many of the finer details so Faith wasn't to worry. This she found mildly irritating, but understood that her superiors were probably just trying to remove any minor pressures, rather than interfering.

As she was wrapping up the conversation, Pat appeared on the path with the Lively sisters in tow, and a couple of buckets of chrysanthemums. Pat conducted the flower arranging with military precision. They were finished in time for the six o'clock news, which, she informed Faith, she never liked to miss.

Faith locked up the church feeling a little as if she had survived a strong wind. Pat was a force of nature.

Darkness was drawing in. Faith paused to admire the pink sky over Shoesmith's farm. This is the evening before Alistair Ingram's funeral, she reminded herself. So much had happened in so few days. She felt off balance; unreal. Through the lime trees she saw a light go on in the vicarage kitchen. She thought of Don's face on the day of Trevor Shoesmith's suicide – was that really only two days ago? Don had stood in almost this exact spot outside the vestry door. *I'm not going in there…*

How was he going to manage the funeral, then?

This was real; she should go and check on the murdered man's son.

The kitchen looked like a brightly lit stage set from the shadowy garden. An empty set. She opened the door and called out. She heard Don saying something to someone and the sound of the front door closing. She waited. He walked back into the kitchen. He looked amused as he saw her.

"Hello!" he greeted her. Inexplicably, he glanced back over his shoulder as if there were someone behind him, but there was no one there.

"Is this a convenient time? I just wanted to check in with you; see how you're doing."

His expression was politely puzzled. "I'm fine."

"How are you feeling – are you going to be OK tomorrow?" She could see that he wasn't going to make this easy for her. Don stared back at her blankly.

"It was my impression you didn't feel comfortable about setting foot in the church," she stated baldly.

"Oh, that's all right!" he responded jauntily. "I don't need to. I'm not going to go to the funeral."

"You're not?"

"No." His face stretched into a stiff smile. "Can I offer you coffee – or something stronger? I fancy a G&T. Oh, before I forget!" He held up a finger, indicating she should wait there, and disappeared into the hall. He re-emerged holding a parcel. "The postman left this. Church supplies of some sort."

It was a box of palm crosses for next Sunday's service.

"Thank you." Faith took the box, her brain whirring. How to handle this? Alistair Ingram's son was clearly in an odd mood, and she didn't know him well.

"I think a gin and tonic would be an excellent thing," she said brightly.

They sipped their drinks in silence, facing one another across the kitchen table. Her drink was long on gin and short on tonic. She felt the liquid seep in, relaxing her muscles. Don was watching her. She had a cartoon vision of him as a big sleek cat and herself as a small brown mouse. He was going to sit her out.

He didn't know how stubborn she could be.

"So, what are your plans?" she asked.

"Plans?"

"After all this. Where will you go?" This vicarage was tied to his father's job. Not much mercy for the orphans of serving clergy. Lose your home and parent in one package. She would be angry if she were him.

He glanced around the spacious kitchen.

"Getting ready to move in?" he asked flatly.

"It does look like a nice house." That took him aback. He almost smiled. "But no. I was actually asking about you."

Don got up to freshen his drink. He took a long swallow.

"I'll be all right. Dad's left me well provided for." He watched her reaction. "He was quite wealthy – but you know that."

He came back to the table and sat down again.

"I've found a flat in Southampton. Convenient for the university. It'll do me for now." He seemed to be challenging her somehow. "Sean's going to be my lodger."

Lucky Sean, she thought. He's fallen on his feet. Don's standards of living were much higher than the normal student could expect.

She examined the handsome, half-formed face across the table. Don sat, his long limbs sprawled, one arm draped along the back of his chair, his free hand rocking his glass on the tabletop. He seemed to be waiting for something. The moment passed.

"So my father's dead and I've come in to a nice inheritance." His eyes fixed hers aggressively.

"Oh! I'm sure you have an alibi," said Faith calmly, and sipped her drink.

He blinked.

"Brilliant!" A grin transformed his face. "Welcome back, Nancy Drew!" He raised his glass to her. "Actually, I don't have one," he resumed. "An alibi. I was here on my own that morning." His eyes defied her to challenge him. "Which fact, as I am sure you will recognize as a student of crime, indicates that I did not poison my father. For being, as I hope you will allow, intelligent," he bowed self-mockingly from the waist, "had I murdered him, I would have provided myself with one – an alibi, that is."

What was he? Nineteen, maybe twenty years old? There he was, utterly alone, his mother long dead, facing eviction from his home and the funeral of his murdered father, and yet he still had the guts to put on this performance. Faith wanted to applaud and cry at the same time.

"But then I suppose," Don struck an exaggeratedly thoughtful pose, "you might say I lost my temper and struck out on a whim. After all, they do say I hated my father."

Faith grimaced. "Not precisely. What I understood was that you quarrelled over certain things."

He pouted, as if he were considering the point. "And sons have been known to dispute things with their fathers," he pointed out.

Peter Gray had said much the same thing.

"How did you feel about your father's engagement to Jessica?" she asked.

"His engagement?"

"Jessica told me your father was going to tell you about it that morning." She didn't need to add which morning. They both knew.

"I saw you," she forestalled his denial, "coming out of the vestry. You looked upset. Your father called after you, but you didn't turn back."

"Don't you get around," he said sulkily. Faith kept her eyes on his – the connection seemed almost physical. To her surprise, he capitulated.

"Yes. He told me."

"And it made you angry?"

"Not really."

It was tiring maintaining this intensity. She hoped she wouldn't lose him.

"You looked angry. So what was the quarrel about?"

"Not that – he was a grown-up. He could marry again if he wanted. I wasn't going to be around much longer anyway."

"If not that, then what?"

He drew air in through his nose with a sharp sniff and folded his arms across his chest.

"Lifestyle choices," he said. "Another drink?"

"Thanks, but that's my limit." She tossed back the last of her drink and stood up.

Oops! That gin and tonic was strong. She steadied herself surreptitiously on the tabletop as she picked up the parcel of palm crosses.

"I should drop these off at the church." She looked at him directly. "Why don't you come with me?"

She glimpsed anxiety flicker across his face. He really wasn't very old.

"Come on, there's nothing to be afraid of," she said quietly. "It's just a place."

He seemed to be listening to something a long way off. Then he pushed back his chair, the legs scraping the floor with a harsh sound. He took the parcel out of her hands.

"OK." He led the way. "But if you're afraid of the dark, why don't you just admit it?" He stepped down into the shadowy garden.

Following him out, Faith's eyes rested on the Georgian satinwood salt box by the door. She remembered the keys hanging inside.

"How are you about locking up when you're not around?" she asked.

"The front door locks itself. Dad was always forgetting his keys."

"So you often leave the back door unlocked?"

She caught the movement of his shoulders as he shrugged in the gloom.

"Crime isn't rife round here. Don't know that anyone locks their back door – unless they're going away."

It was really quite dark under the trees. She didn't remember the ground being this rough.

"We should have brought a torch."

"Wait a minute, your eyes will adjust." His voice was surprisingly close. "The sky's clear tonight."

They'd stopped. All of a sudden, she was conscious of his breathing. His presence was an outline in the dark.

"I can't prove I loved Dad," he said, "but I did."

St James's Church loomed on the other side of the trees, a solid presence between them and the night sky.

"Why should I go tomorrow?" Don seemed to be talking to himself. "It's their funeral."

"It's your father's funeral."

"He's not there any more."

He was crying in the dark. She could feel his struggle to regain control. She took a step towards him. He flung out a hand.

"Don't! I'm OK." He sniffed. "Just angry." She saw the line of his shoulders rise as he straightened up. "Let them take him. They took him away a long time ago."

"Is that really how you feel about it?"

He shifted restlessly.

"He was a perfectly normal guy and then Mum died and he got sucked in. They got him when he was vulnerable."

"He changed from the man you knew?"

"Not exactly. Well, sort of. It was like he had discovered this great secret. Overnight he changed everything, and I had to tag along. We left London. And I'm suddenly the *vicar's son*," he put savage quotes around the phrase, "in the back-end of nowhere… And now he's dead and he had to die in there," he ended despairingly.

Faith was angry with herself. She knew she should have fought harder to make Canon Matthews and the bishop pay more attention to Ingram's son. Instead, she'd let them take over the funeral with hardly a protest. She hadn't given Don the support he deserved.

"They're the ones burying Dad tomorrow. It doesn't matter if I'm there or not," Don muttered.

"Yes it does. It matters for you." She thought of Bishop Anthony and the rural dean. They would be appalled if they knew how Alistair's son felt. She reached out and rubbed his arm. Half a second later, she realized what she was doing and that Don hadn't pulled away. Perhaps she was making progress.

"I might as well be invisible," she heard him mumble.

"Jessica feels the same way," Faith murmured. Damn! Did I say that aloud?

"What?"

His tone was outraged. She kicked herself for being so unguarded. Of course, at this stage of grief he would see it as a contest.

"I know Jessica was new to your father's life," she said, loading her voice with as much sympathy as she could without sounding too sickly and false. "But they loved one another – she is mourning his loss too. Maybe," she suggested tentatively, "if you give it time, you will find a bit of comfort in one another."

She could feel the tension in him.

"It is not the same," she added hurriedly, "but there is a way in which you both have your father in common."

He grunted. She couldn't read his face; it was in shadow. She'd been here before. Ever since she'd committed herself to spreading the word that God's love was for all, she seemed destined to run up against non-believers to whom church represented only bitter exclusion. She stumbled on.

"Bishop Beech and the rest, they're trying to express their respect for your father. Whatever your personal perspective, he was very popular here. He did good work and was appreciated as a good man. You should be proud of that. And you need to be there tomorrow," she said earnestly. She thought of her own father's funeral – what she could remember of it, which wasn't much. "You'll feel better for it afterwards."

"Yeah?"

"Yeah," she nodded emphatically.

They'd reached the vestry door. She took out her keys, squinting at them in the poor light to find the right one.

"When did you last go inside? Not just the vestry, the church itself?" she asked.

"I don't remember."

She opened the vestry door and turned on the lights. "Come on then, deep breath."

They crossed the vestry and entered the nave.

"I hate this place," he said passionately. "I can't breathe in here."

"Why?" She thought she knew the answer, but he needed to talk about it.

"Everything," he swept his hand out. "All this brass and dark wood and coloured glass; they're nothing but magic props – staging to sustain a delusion."

A woman past thirty falling for this delusion – for what? Faith gave herself a little shake. She wished Ben would get out of her head.

"Did your father seem deluded? Was he unhappy?" she asked.

Don glanced down at her. His expression was vivid with intelligence.

"Many deluded people are deliriously happy. That's a sign of delusion, isn't it?"

She acknowledged the point.

"And that's how your father struck you?"

He stood staring at the altar and the cross above it a moment.

"No," he said finally. "He seemed at peace with himself."

She showed him the place where his father died, and talked about the good things she had learned about Alistair Ingram in the last week. Don seemed to listen. After a while, he struck her as calmer; a little less tense.

They walked past the stained-glass panel and its smiling Lamb of God.

"I thought that had gone," he commented idly.

"What do you mean?"

"Oh, I let a man in the other day – I thought he was from the glass company."

Faith felt a sudden shot of adrenaline. "What day was that?"

Don thought about it. "Saturday."

"Last Saturday?"

"Yes, I was listening to the match on the radio and he interrupted. I gave him the key to get rid of him." He walked on towards the door.

"Did he say he was from the glass company?"

"I'm not sure he did. I just assumed."

"Did you often give the key out like that?"

"If I was in and Dad was out and they had a good reason to be there. The glass guys had been around for weeks. Restoration works."

"So you would know them by sight?"

He glanced down at her, amused. He shook his head. "I paid as little attention as possible."

"What can you remember about that particular man last Saturday? What did he look like?"

"Middling – middle-aged, middle height."

She gave him a severe look. Don rolled his eyes. He ran his fingers through his thick hair.

"Not much on top," he elaborated, "brownish to fair; not bald but close-cropped like guys do when the hair's going. Tanned, like he worked outdoors." He shrugged.

"Anything else?" she insisted.

"Not really."

"Nothing else? Just middling, light brown cropped hair and tanned?" she said, trying to keep the frustration from her voice.

"He rocked," Don said as an afterthought. "When he moved. It wasn't that pronounced, but he had a limp."

Her initial excitement gradually subsided. She turned off the lights and locked up. They were talking about the Saturday. It had already been proved that the poison was put in the cruet on the day Ingram drank the wine: the next day, the Sunday. On the other hand, Don's revelations did suggest that the security at St James's wasn't the best. She thought of the satinwood key box and the unlocked back door.

"A man with a limp!" Don looked sideways at her. Even in the dim light she caught his cynical expression. "There! We have a suspect. Doesn't that sound like a murderer?"

CHAPTER
16

THE ALARM BEEPED INSISTENTLY in the darkness. The radio clicked on.

This is the seven o'clock news...

She'd better wake up, then. But it was warm in bed and her eyelids just didn't want to open.

A British aid worker is missing... Rift Valley Province...

What? Faith sat up, staring at the radio as if the sight of it would make her ears sharper. She waited impatiently as the announcer completed the headlines. Her fingers played with the sheet of paper by the bed, where she'd been going over her wording for the funeral later.

Concern is rising for a British aid worker missing in Tanzania. The alarm was raised when the woman, employed as a health worker at the Stonefree Refugee Camp, failed to return from a two-week leave. Tensions in the area are high after a series of clashes between the local population and refugees over accusations of illegal hunting...

Celia Beech! Faith thought of the bishop's wife sitting alone at the café table by the fogged window. Poor Alison! She had the uneasy feeling this day wasn't going to get any better. She swung her legs out of bed.

Downstairs, Ruth was already up and dressed. She was ironing clothes from a loaded laundry basket at her feet. She refused Faith's offer of coffee.

"Had breakfast already," she said. Her words were clipped. "I've decided to drive up to Birmingham to spend the weekend with Mum. It's Auntie Jean's birthday. You know how she's been after to me to visit."

She was ironing a blouse as if she would like to rub it out. Auntie Jean was Ruth's godmother, one of their mother's oldest friends and a principal reason for Marianne's move back to the city of her birth. Faith took a sip of coffee. Ruth had a special bond with her godmother, but why the sudden decision? And on a Friday?

"What about work?"

"I've told them I'm taking one of my days. I've plenty stacked up." Ruth ground the iron into a cuff. "That 'vision' woman is getting right up my nose and she's running a workshop today."

Faith hugged the warm coffee mug to her chest.

"So you've decided to get out of it for a while."

"Mmm." Ruth put the blouse on a hanger and hung it up. She took a skirt from the mound in the laundry basket and gave the fabric a savage tug, straightening it on the board. "Sean's not come to visit," she sniffed.

"He's staying with a friend – with Don," Faith said.

"I bet he's seen his father though," said Ruth.

Faith put the mug down, and walked behind her sister. She put a hand against her lower back and kissed her on the cheek. "He's a good boy," she said. "And he loves you."

Ruth turned her face away to look at the clock behind her.

"You'd better get going," she said. "You've got that funeral this morning, haven't you?"

It was close to nine, Faith saw. George Casey, the diocesan press officer, had left her two voicemails already warning her to get to the church early. The press were gathering and he wanted her there for a "briefing". Ruth was right; she needed to get a move on.

The green was crowded with vehicles. She turned into Shoesmith's lane. Her phone rang. It was the bishop's press officer.

"Where are you?" Casey demanded. His voice was charged with excitement.

"Just parking."

"Don't come in round the front of the vicarage. Come in the back way."

"Journalists?"

"Haven't you seen the papers?"

"Haven't had time this morning."

"We're all across the tabloids," he said impatiently, and rang off.

Faith looked at the phone. Oops! Her battery was on its last two bars. She made a mental note: must charge phone tonight.

She made her way past the church and through the lime trees. There was a uniformed constable posted in the vicarage garden. They acknowledged one another with a nod of the head.

"Watch out for the snappers," he said.

"Journos in the shrubbery?"

"We're trying to hold them at the front, but I've chased three out already," he shrugged, resigned. "Mr Ingram's been advised he'd do best to stay away from windows as much as possible."

"This is going to be fun," she quipped. The constable responded with a lugubrious grin.

George Casey was hovering in the kitchen as she climbed the steps. He barely waited for the customary exchange of greetings.

"Just wanted to catch you before I went out front." His eyes never rested on her face but darted about the room, words pattering out of his mouth at speed. "If you get cornered, don't mention murder. We're calling it heart failure... Great loss to the diocese. Condolences to the family; don't wish to comment further on an ongoing investigation – that sort of thing. If we're not careful, this story is going to run for weeks. All we've got coming up is the bishop's Easter sermon..." His gaze paused thoughtfully mid-air. "Of course, that'll have to be revised..."

He spun round on his heel and left her. She heard him open the front door and a burst of sound as he stepped outside into bright light and a clamour of questions. The door slammed shut.

In the front room, the curtains were closed and the lights were on. Don sat with his back to her in a stylish modern recliner. Sean was looking in the mirror, straightening his tie. They were both correctly dressed in dark suits. She felt a rush of warmth: he was coming, then.

"Good morning," she said.

"Aunt Faith." Sean came over and gave her a hug.

"How's he doing?" she murmured.

"Holding up."

"No need to whisper," Don said, coming over to join them. He surprised her by leaning in and kissing her on the cheek. "Why don't we make a move while that annoying little man is feeding the news hounds?"

"I'll get the others," Sean said, taking out his mobile phone.

"Others?" she queried.

"Some friends have come down from Southampton – to give support. I thought if we all walked round Don, we could give him some cover from all that lot." He jerked his head in the direction of the front door and the press beyond it.

"Good thinking, Batman." Faith brushed a piece of lint off his collar, feeling particularly proud of her nephew. He was such a caring, sensible lad.

"I'm Robin," he shot back, twinkling at her.

The Southampton friends proved to be a varied group. Sean introduced Faith to a chunky middle-aged woman with a weather-beaten face and wistful eyes.

"This is Wendy. She runs our favourite bar." They shook hands. Wendy had a powerful grip. "Alice and Mike," Sean continued, indicating a jolly-looking girl whose rosy cheeks suggested an outdoor life, and a willowy boy in cords. "That's Jude," he went on. A dab of a girl with spiky hair dyed black and wearing aggressive eyeliner dug her hands in her pockets, shrinking deeper inside the over-large black coat she wore; she seemed faintly worried. "And this is Sol."

Sol was small and sleek and olive-skinned. He wore a beautifully cut black suit that might have been Armani, and a silver stud in one ear.

"I am pleased to meet you," he addressed Faith formally. His accent sounded Spanish or possibly Argentinian. "I am Cath-o-lic," he informed her solemnly.

The front door opened and Peter Gray slipped in.

"Hearse is on its way," he said. He leaned in to Faith and murmured, "The rural dean was asking after you."

She looked at her watch. She still had plenty of time to get into full service rig.

"I should be going," she said.

"We'll look after him," Sean assured her. "See you out front."

They formed a phalanx around Don. Peter Gray opened the door. Faith sensed as much as saw the scrum of journalists and photographers beyond. Then they were swallowed up.

She found Canon Matthews and the bishop already robed in the vestry. Mrs Beech stood by the door in a tweed suit that made her look a generation out of place.

"Forgive me. I was checking on Don Ingram," Faith pulled the surplice over her cassock. She adjusted the black funeral stole, making sure it lay flat around her neck. She looked around for her hymnal and order of service.

"How is he?" asked Canon Matthews, handing them to her.

"He'll do. Police say the hearse is on its way."

"I shall go and find a seat," Alison told her husband.

Faith detained the older woman with a hand on her sleeve.

"I am so sorry to hear the news this morning," she said. Alison looked over her shoulder and nodded. Her eyes were red-rimmed. "You are all in my prayers. And your son – how's Simon holding up?"

"He's still down in Lymington." Alison almost sounded cross. "With all the press – we don't want them to bother him."

Alison's mouth was tense. Faith wondered if she regretted their café encounter. Perhaps she felt she had been too unguarded. Bishop Beech intervened.

"You'll understand, unfortunately with everything going on, Alison and I will have to slip away smart-ish after the service. I hope you can explain to young Donald."

"Of course." Faith watched Alison disappear into the body of the church. She caught a glimpse of Pat directing mourners, and then the door shut.

There was quite a crowd outside the church gate. Don stood with Sean beside him and their friends to either side. The hearse advanced slowly towards them, the funeral director walking before it in his traditional garb, the top hat with weepers, and mourning gloves covering his hands.

"Very moving," said a voice.

She turned to find a bland-faced young man with the compact body of a footballer standing at her shoulder.

"Excuse me?"

"Andy Baine, Grundy Agency," he said, and bent one arm from the elbow as if offering to shake hands. She noticed he had a reporter's notebook palmed in the other hand. "Reporter. Perhaps we could have a word…"

They were getting ready to bring the coffin out.

"I'm sorry, you'll have to excuse me. I need to be inside to receive the coffin."

Andy gestured with a little flick of his hand. A photographer pushed forward, his camera snapping in Don's face. Before she could react, a small determined figure interposed itself. Pat waved her plump hands before the lens, ruining the shot.

"What *do* you think you're doing?" she exclaimed, her voice vibrant with disgust.

Inside the church, every pew was filled. Faith took her place before the altar beside Bishop Anthony and Canon Matthews, ready to receive the coffin. Bishop Anthony was wearing his mitre and robes and carrying his crook. The vestments were embroidered in vivid modern designs. A mitre really doesn't suit the human head, Faith reflected. Brass and coloured glass. What if they were right – Ben and Don; what if it was a delusion and all this just set-dressing?

Her eyes alighted on Jessica sitting beside Fred. They were surrounded by Clarisse and Timothy, Sue and a man who must be her husband, and the Lively sisters. Pat slipped into the seat behind Fred. The coffin was at the door. Every head turned back to watch. Such disparate people sitting together, and each one watching Don walk behind his father's coffin. The compassion on their faces gave them a fleeting family resemblance. There is more to this than mere delusion, Faith thought.

The coffin was getting nearer. Something was wrong. Don had paused yards from the front pew. Faith's breath froze in her lungs. He wouldn't... He had seemed fine half an hour ago. She glimpsed Sean in perplexed profile.

Don Ingram turned on his heel and headed back against the flow of mourners behind him. He couldn't leave; not now!

He took a couple of strides and stopped. He was looking down at Jessica Rose. Time stood still. He stretched out an arm, his hand open towards her. Jessica got to her feet. Arm in arm in silence they walked together to the front pew. Don waited for Jessica to take her seat and then sat down beside her, Sean and his friends falling into place around them.

Breath whispered between her lips and her shoulders relaxed. Faith was overtaken by a rush of hope.

That didn't go too badly. Faith stripped off her cassock and packed it away. She was glad to have the vestry to herself. She needed a moment to catch her breath. Bishop Anthony and his wife had already left. Alistair Ingram's body was on its way to the crematorium where Canon Matthews was to hold a small private ceremony for Don and a few friends later in the day. She straightened her hair in the fly-spotted mirror on the vestry wall. She should find Jessica and take her home.

She went out by the vestry door. The clematis draped across the wall was past its best. Petals scattered the gravel. Her feet followed the path as if they had trod it for years. But she'd been here less than a week. She had a dizzying moment of awareness, and then her reality steadied again. Jessica. She needed to care for Jessica.

The woman Alistair Ingram had loved was standing by Fred, her eyes cast down, in a world of her own. She looked utterly defeated.

Andy Baine detached himself from a knot of mourners by a yew tree and stepped into Faith's path.

"Is that the dead man's intended, Mrs Rose?" he said, nodding in Jessica's direction.

"Please, not now." Faith gestured towards George Casey doing a stand-up for the local TV station by the gate. "You need to speak to the diocesan press officer; he's handling all press enquiries."

Peter Gray's comforting shape seemed to appear out of nowhere. Faith wondered if he had been keeping an eye on her.

"My hero," she murmured as he took charge of the journalist. He responded with a sheepish grin.

"Mr Baine," Peter said jauntily. "Let me show you the way."

If the press were onto Jessica, it was definitely time to get her away. Faith considered where she had parked her car. The press pack was thick at the church gate. Perhaps the best thing would be to drive round to the front of the vicarage and have Fred bring Jessica through that way.

She retrieved her car without incident and positioned it facing down the drive before the house. The front door was unlocked. She opened it and went in. As she passed the front room, she glanced in. The curtains were still drawn. In the dim light she saw Don. He was sitting on the couch, his shoulders shuddering as he sobbed.

Faith heard Fred call her name. She saw him standing at the gate to the vicarage, so normal and familiar even in his funeral suit.

"There you are. Jessica's ready to go home."

"Of course." Faith forced a smile. Sean had come into the lounge, and held out a box of tissues to his friend. She smiled sadly; she wasn't needed here.

"I'm parked outside the church. Let's get going."

CHAPTER

FAITH DROVE MECHANICALLY. Beside her in the passenger seat, Jessica leaned back with her eyes closed. Faith felt loose and detached. It was almost like being drunk. This was no good. She was in charge of a moving vehicle and a grieving would-be widow. She focused on the road before her.

Somehow she found her way back to Jessica's. The cottage stood on a curving, semi-rural lane. Faith slowed down.

"Almost home," she said.

Jessica opened her eyes. There was a police car parked on the street and another car parked in the drive behind Jessica's own silver saloon. Next to them stood a middle-aged woman with greying hair, a uniformed constable, and Ben.

"What's Di doing here?" asked Jessica. Faith belatedly recognized the neighbour whom she'd met when she'd brought Jessica home the last time, the day of Trevor Shoesmith's suicide.

Ben approached the car. He waited for them to get out.

"I am sorry, Mrs Rose, but there seems to have been a break-in."

"A break-in?" Jessica echoed. Di put an arm around her.

"Oh, my dear, I'm so sorry – on this day of all days. I was upstairs cleaning and I looked out and there was this man climbing out of your side window – you know, the living room one by the kitchen? I didn't get much of a look at him. I opened the window and bellowed and he dropped out of sight. He must have been parked in the lane because I heard a car start up. But I couldn't see anything because of the hedge."

Faith saw Ben jerk his head at her. She followed him round the side of the house.

"Jemmied," he said, pointing to a casement standing ajar. A police technician in overalls was inside, brushing for fingerprints. He glanced up and Faith recognized him from earlier in the week.

"Why are you here?" she asked Ben. "Burglaries are hardly your usual beat."

"Got the heads-up when Jessica Rose's name came up."

"You think this may be connected?"

Faith tried to summon up some enthusiasm, but she was finding it hard to concentrate. Ben glanced at her impatiently.

"Just got here."

"Any useful description?"

Ben shook his head. "The neighbour didn't get much of a look – she was standing at that window up there." He pointed over to Di's house. "With the hedge in the way, she only got a glimpse looking down on the top of his head. Short brown to fair hair. Probably thirties to forties, but she can't be sure."

"Thirties to forties – wouldn't you expect an opportunistic break-in to be committed by someone younger?" she asked. Ben shrugged.

"Too early to tell."

They joined the others.

"Can I ask you to make a tour of the house, Mrs Rose, to see if you notice anything missing?" Ben asked.

For a moment, Faith thought Jessica hadn't heard him. She stood stock-still, her fair hair bright against her dark coat. Then she nodded her head once, as if confirming something to herself, and led the way into the house.

They followed her from room to room. The living room, a study, the kitchen and a downstairs bathroom. The cottage was neat. Jessica, it seemed, wasn't one for clutter. They filed up the stairs in silence. Faith had an illogical desire to giggle. It was such an odd house tour. They peered inside a bright guest room with polished board floor and sunflower yellow accents. Nothing. No sign of any disturbance. Nothing out of place. They came to the master bedroom.

There was a creamware jug dashed with modernistic slashes in purples and pinks on the bedside table. It was filled with irises. The colours stood out against the room's limewashed furniture and pale fabrics. Faith had seen that jug before. She'd noticed it when she'd brought Jessica back earlier in the week. It had stood on a windowsill in the hall. There, against the crisp white paint, it had looked good. Here it was out of place, its colours brash in the muted underwater elegance of the bedroom. Jessica must be upset to have done that, she thought.

The bedding was white with a slim Regency stripe in a pale jade. It was rumpled, the duvet thrown back as if Jessica had just climbed out of it. There was a glint of silver in the creased bottom sheet. Jessica pulled the duvet up over the mess.

"I didn't have time to tidy up this morning," she murmured.

Ben came up beside her. She watched him, fascinated, as he leaned past her to turn back the cover. He straightened up with a thread of silver hanging from his fingers. It was a chain, and attached to it was a pendant in the shape of a simple fish – the Christian symbol.

"What's this?" he asked.

There was a pause – only a fraction of a second.

"That's where it was; I thought I'd lost it – the clasp must have broken loose." Jessica took it from him and folded it into her hand.

Faith visualized Jessica as she had been the day before – the simple black dress with its scoop neck. She was certain that chain hadn't been around her neck. She'd never seen it before. Perhaps it's from Alistair, she thought, and Jessica keeps it under her pillow. That's why she is embarrassed.

Jessica led the way to the door.

"I don't see anything missing." Jessica's voice was a little loud. "Di probably disturbed the intruder on his way in, and he didn't manage to get anything."

"The witness described the man as climbing *out* of the window." Ben contemplated her gravely.

Jessica flushed under his gaze. She looked away, and led them down the stairs.

"Well, I can't see anything. I have window locks – it's my fault; I stopped using them. I can secure the window. I shall be more careful in future. I shall be fine."

She had reached the bottom of the staircase. She paused, looking back up at them. She seemed anxious to be rid of them. What's she worried about? Faith wondered.

Ben was lifting his eyebrows in his most quizzical expression.

"I… I've been told the police don't have much chance of catching a casual burglar like this," Jessica murmured.

"But we still make the attempt, Mrs Rose," Ben responded blandly.

A policewoman came to the front door. She seemed vaguely amused.

"We've found another witness, sir."

"Who?"

The policewoman took them outside. A small boy, maybe eleven years old, stood holding a bicycle.

"This is Richard Shelley," the policewoman said. "He lives at number nineteen, across the way. Richard, this is the inspector in charge of the case – Inspector Shorter."

The side of Richard's face was bruised and swollen. Faith had a sudden lurch of alarm then she suppressed it. How cynical had she become, to think of abuse the moment she saw a bruise on a child? The boy's eyes and hair shone. His clothes were clean and of good quality. Ben acknowledged him with a nod.

"Why aren't you in school?"

"Been to the dentist," Richard responded confidently. He didn't seem in the least wary of adults.

"What happened to you?" Faith asked.

"George B and me we was practising hammer-throwing at break – with our bags. His strap broke." Richard enthusiastically pantomimed an object hitting him in the face. "And it hit me full on!"

"Poor you! That must've hurt," Faith exclaimed sympathetically.

"Broke my tooth," Richard told her proudly.

"Did you keep the piece?" she enquired. The corner of Ben's mouth twitched.

Richard nodded.

"Got it in a matchbox. It's in my bedroom. Want to see?"

"Maybe later."

"So what can you tell us about what you saw earlier?" Ben resumed control of the conversation. "You were riding your bike?"

"That way," Richard pointed down the street, "and I heard this car drive off really fast. The tyres screeched."

"What did it look like?"

"I didn't see it exactly."

"You didn't see it?"

"There was the hedge."

"But you heard it."

"Yeah. It sounded like it needed a tune-up; it wasn't running right. I think the timing was out," he pronounced with an authoritative air.

"The timing?" Ben queried with a straight face.

"Or something. It was making a noise." Richard made a throaty noise, a cross between a growl and a cough. "Like that."

Behind them, Jessica was restless. One moment she was picking at the lapel of her coat, the next she was biting the edge of her thumb.

"Would you prefer to go and wait with Di?" Faith asked her. "The police will be here a bit longer yet."

"No. I'll stay here." Jessica went back inside the house and sank down onto a chair in the living room. "You really don't need to stay," she said sharply. She glanced up at Faith. "It's been a long day." Her mouth moved in a shadow of a smile.

Faith realized just how tired she was herself. She'd had enough. She wanted to get home and have a cup of tea and some solitude.

"If you're sure? You have my number if you need anything."

Jessica nodded. Faith left her there, sitting in her straight-backed chair, her fingers twisting together in her lap.

Ben was sitting in his car, talking on the radio. Faith told the policewoman she was leaving and got into her car. A boxy black jeep had drawn up in the street. Andy Baine got out, notebook in hand. He called out.

"Reverend Morgan! If you have a moment…"

That's all she needed. She kept her head down and fumbled her key into the ignition. The engine purred into life. Andy Baine returned to his own car.

She wasn't sure what happened next. Her car leapt forward and she swung the steering wheel, heading out into the road. There was a loud bang and the sound of breaking glass.

The black and chrome nose of the jeep was towering over the side of her little blue car. She felt fresh air on her face. Across the metal of her oddly canted bonnet, she could see Andy Baine's face through the starred glass of his windscreen. He looked outraged. Her hands seemed locked onto the steering wheel in front of her. She looked down at them. With a great effort she peeled the fingers of her right hand open and turned off the ignition. Silence hummed in her head. There was glass everywhere and her neck hurt. She put a hand up to her forehead. Her fingers touched wet. There was blood on her hand.

The car door was wrenched open. Ben was crouching in the gap. He seemed to be saying something urgent. She was glad to see him.

"What happened?" she asked.

"Are you all right?" He reached out and cupped her face with his hands, looking into her eyes. She could see the charcoal ring around his iris. She'd always envied him his lashes. They were way too good for a man.

She wriggled cautiously, testing out her limbs and neck. All present and correct – just about.

Ben was holding a white handkerchief. He dabbed her forehead. His touch was gentle.

"It's just a scratch. You'll be OK," he said. "Out you come..."

She swung her legs obediently out of the car and he helped her up. She leaned into him. He was nice and steady. He brushed pellets of shattered glass from her skirt.

"My car!" Faith almost cried. The pretty sky-blue bonnet was crumpled and the windscreen was gone. The front left wheel leaned into the road at an odd angle. Andy Baine stood on the pavement with the policewoman and her colleague on either side. His habitual confidence seemed to have taken a knock.

"Journo! What the hell was he thinking?" Ben cursed.

Faith flinched. His grip on her upper arm was uncomfortable. She was startled by his anger.

"Come on. I'm taking you home before I..." He steered her away.

"But the car..." Faith couldn't take her eyes off it.

"Leave your insurance details with the PC and they'll get it sorted."

The policewoman approached them.

"Sir – what..."

Ben cut her short.

"I don't want to deal with him," he said emphatically. "Charge him if you can, but I'm taking Ms Morgan home."

CHAPTER
18

THEY PARKED IN FRONT OF RUTH'S plastic-coated front door. Faith felt too tired to move. She ached. Ben opened the passenger door.

"Out you come." He hauled her to her feet. She let him take charge, resisting the urge to bury her face in his jacket. "Where are the keys?"

She found them in her bag. He took them from her, opened the door and followed her in.

"OK. Where does big sister keep the booze? We need a drink."

It didn't seem real. Ben was standing here in Ruth's dinky little front room. He moved towards the kitchen.

"I'll just have tea," she said, going after him.

Ben filled the kettle, and she watched him opening cupboards and drawers. He produced two mugs, and dropped tea bags into each. In the past, he'd have had a beer, and she appreciated the show of solidarity.

"Sit."

She flopped onto the sofa as the kettle boiled and he made the tea, handing a mug to her. Ben sat beside her and blew across the top of his.

"I've an appointment with the bishop in the morning."

She blinked. But poor Bishop Anthony had so much

to deal with already.

"Why?"

"Pesticide."

The cogs in her brain struggled to mesh.

"You don't seriously think…?"

"Check everything. I've got to follow the pesticide."

She remembered what Luke McIvor had told them about decanting a bottle of pesticide for the bishop's roses. She saw Alison Beech averting her red-rimmed eyes when she spoke to her hours earlier. Could she know something? She shook her head. It was absurd.

"But there is no possible motive that might involve Bishop Anthony," she exclaimed irritably. It felt good to have a legitimate outlet for the loose energy swirling through her.

"Offended that Ingram was letting the side down in some way…?" Ben suggested. She could tell he wasn't convinced.

"That's reaching!" she scoffed. "You're not seriously telling me you'd entertain the idea for one minute that Bishop Beech might have murdered Alistair Ingram?"

Ben gazed back at her blandly. He was just being stubborn. He never did like to back down.

"So who's your favourite, then? Dazzle me."

That was bullish, even for him. Was he being deliberately annoying? She took a sip of tea.

"What's been bugging me…"

"Ye-es," prompted Ben facetiously.

She ignored him, absorbed in her own line of thought.

"It was the combination of Ingram's heart problem and the poison that killed him – not the pesticide alone. So can we assume the poisoner knew about his heart?"

"If they meant to kill him."

"Perhaps," she waved his objection aside, "but if you assume the intention was to kill…"

Beside her, she felt Ben shift his position. He was watching her think.

"It was Pat Montesque who first mentioned Ingram's dicky heart to me almost the moment we met..."

Ben inclined his head in a slow nod.

"Planting doubts about his health." Faith recalled Pat's expression that first day. *He looks wonderfully well, but...* "She also mentioned finances. In her first few sentences she said he had a 'dicky heart' and he was good with finances." She sat up. "Did you know that Ingram was involved in a financial fraud just before he made his career change to the church? Well," she corrected herself, trying to be fair, "tangentially at least."

She scanned Ben's face, trying to read his expression. Was she reporting old news?

"That case went to court," he responded coolly. "There was nothing to suggest Alistair Ingram was anything but an innocent bystander."

She should have known. Ben was always thorough. She didn't want to give up so easily.

"One of the congregation told me that a few years back Pat had financial troubles. What if Pat was one of the victims of the fraud somehow – or knew something about it?"

"Blackmail? For what? Ingram was a witness for the prosecution in that case. He helped bring the fraudsters to account. Just because she knew about his dodgy heart, Mrs Montesque, churchwarden and respected pillar of the community, planted poison in the communion wine to kill a Good Samaritan? Really?"

He was laughing at her. Faith flushed with annoyance. He didn't have to be that dismissive. She wasn't aware of the details of the case. She'd only had rumours to work with; she didn't have his access to legal archives. She took an angry gulp of scalding tea and regretted it.

She thought of Sue's passing reference to Pat blossoming after the death of her invalid husband. What if Little Worthy green was sheltering a serial poisoner?

"Oh, come on!" Ben's derision broke in on her musings. "You're supposed to be a good judge of character! You don't really see that woman as a murderer?"

Faith thought of Pat's defence of Don when the photographer was intrusive outside the church, and the compassion on her face as she watched him walk behind his father's coffin. Did she really think that badly of Pat Montesque? She wasn't certain of anything any more.

"All right," she admitted crossly. "But I still think Ingram's mysterious visits to Pat's house on the green are worth looking into."

"What's that?" He sounded interested now. She felt a smidgen of unworthy satisfaction.

"It was something I was told by a member of the congregation. Alistair Ingram used to call in on Pat at her home – always at the same time."

"She was his churchwarden."

"And so was Fred. But he wasn't at those meetings."

"Maybe they were friends."

"Maybe she was blackmailing him," she shot back.

He leaned forward, his forearms resting on his knees. "For what? Alistair Ingram comes up squeaky clean." He finished his tea and put down the mug. "There was something not right about Mrs Rose today, though."

"Up in the bedroom?" asked Faith eagerly.

"You picked up on it?"

"It was those flowers," Faith agreed, her thoughts tumbling out. "The jug – the colours clashed. It was all wrong – Jessica has way too much good taste for that. It wasn't like her at all."

"What jug?" Ben frowned at her. "It was the pendant. Mrs Rose said she'd lost it – that the clasp had broken. But there was no damage to the clasp. The chain was fastened. It couldn't have fallen off – so what was it doing there?"

"I thought perhaps it was a love token from Alistair Ingram – that's something she might keep under her pillow," she suggested.

He pulled a face. He always had been uncomfortable

with sentimentality.

"Love token!" he joked. "You've been watching too many period dramas." He leaned back, loosening his tie. He stretched out his legs. He looked thinner than she remembered him.

"Have you been losing weight? Are you eating properly?" she asked without thinking. She was caught by the directness of his gaze.

"Why do you care?"

She hadn't meant to get intimate.

"You know I care about you," she murmured, trying to make light of it.

He wouldn't look away.

"Yeah?"

She didn't know what to say. He relented.

"I eat. As it happens," he got up from the sofa in one fluid movement without using his hands, "I am starving right now."

He went into the kitchen where Ruth had a selection of takeaway menus pinned up by the fridge. Faith found she was mesmerized by the line of his back.

"Pizza?"

Probably a bad idea. Her stomach growled. But she was hungry. She hadn't eaten all day.

He took off his jacket, and picked up the phone. He cradled the receiver against his shoulder as he hung his coat over the back of a dining chair and tugged the shoulders straight. It was such a familiar Ben gesture. He was careful about his clothes.

"Pepperoni and peppers, right?"

"You hate peppers."

"But you don't."

He finished the call and put the phone down.

"They say fifteen minutes."

"It's more often twenty," she corrected, just to be saying something. Was he going to come and sit back down beside her, she wondered? This could be a mistake.

Ben leaned against the wall, his hands in his pockets. He

looked down at her with his head tilted back.

"Have I mentioned the gun?" he asked.

"What gun?"

"Shoesmith had a current shotgun licence and the weapon's gone missing."

"That's worrying."

"Mildly," he responded sarcastically, and pushed himself off the wall.

"Who could have taken it?"

"And when was it taken?" Ben capped her. He started to pace and then stopped. Ruth's living room wasn't really big enough for pacing and he had long legs. "For all we know, it could have gone walkabout months ago. The annual check was due next month. It's not as if we have many witnesses to Trevor Shoesmith's life."

He came back and sat down at the opposite end of the sofa, his arms sprawled out along the back.

"What about those friends he stayed with on the weekend Alistair Ingram died?" asked Faith.

"More pub acquaintances than friends. They don't know anything about a shotgun."

"But if Trevor Shoesmith had a gun that day, wouldn't he have used it?" Faith objected. "On the dog, on himself? That sounds as if it had gone missing earlier."

"Perhaps. On the other hand, when we first interviewed Jessica Rose, she suggested that Shoesmith didn't like guns. She implied he didn't have one."

"Did you ask her directly?"

"Hadn't turned up the licence at that point."

Faith was back again in that terrible moment, looking up at a body hanging in the dim light. She shivered. Why should she think of Richard Fisher now? It must be the parallels with Shoesmith's wasted life – and being here with Ben…

She didn't want to think about that.

Ben was watching her sideways; his long lashes were marked against the blue of his eyes.

"I wondered why that barn," she said suddenly, and cleared her throat.

"It was where his brother died," said Ben. His voice was even, professionally devoid of emotion. "Trevor was a fifteen-year-old showing off – he was parking the tractor, lost control. He crushed his brother. It was messy. The boy died of his injuries two days later."

"What utter misery." Faith was baffled by the devastating consequences of simple human frailty, the incremental consequences of bad choices made in a moment.

Sin shall not have dominion over you. How could that be true? The tragedy of that one moment of boyish recklessness had had dominion over poor Trevor. And one moment of Ben's reckless anger had led to the annihilation of Richard Fisher – the consequences of that still had dominion over the both of them.

Ben shrugged.

"It happens."

She looked at the man beside her – every line of his face, the texture of his hair, the shape of his hands; they were all so familiar to her. Yet there was this intractable point between them: Ben who thought of God and redemption as childish fantasy; she, the woman who had given up so much to live by that belief.

Then again, if she really believed that "sin shall not have dominion over you", shouldn't she forgive him?

The sound of the doorbell brought her back to earth.

"I'll get it," said Ben.

She fetched plates and paper napkins and set them out on the coffee table in front of the sofa. The paper napkins were left over from Christmas, sprays of vivid crimson poinsettias against a gold background. No need to be uncivilized just because you're eating with your fingers, she thought.

Ben came back with two pizza boxes and set them on the table. He rolled back the sleeves of his white shirt. His phone rang in his jacket.

"Sorry. Got to take this."

She opened the first box, and a whiff of pepperoni met her, redolent of indulgence and chemical taste enhancers. The other box was Ben's: plain cheese and tomato. Straightforward and uncomplicated. Just how he liked it.

Ben put his mobile away. He fished a bottle of wine from the fridge, and two glasses.

"Budge up."

He sat down next to her. The coffee table wasn't that large. They had to sit close. She was conscious of the pressure of his leg against hers. She resisted the urge to widen the space between them. I'm making too much of this, she scolded herself.

"That was the tech. He's got a nice clean print from Mrs Rose's window, but no match on the local databases."

"So that rules out the usual suspects?" She took a bite into hot cheese goo and spicy pepperoni. The crust was just right. Crunchy and delicious. Ben's mouth was full. He shrugged and swallowed.

"Another loose end." He leaned over her to select another slice. "This whole case is nothing but loose ends. You'd have thought, wouldn't you, that when a vicar is cut down during the Sunday service in front of his flock, the culprit would stand out? But oh, no!"

"What, you expect Christians to be different?"

He looked at her, with a faintly perplexed expression.

"Well, yes. I suppose I did. This God changed you."

"What do you mean?"

"Oh, I don't know," he said with an impatient gesture. "You know. Higher standards. Something better than the rest of us."

"Priggish, you mean?" she quipped, trying to turn the moment.

He leaned back, stretching one arm along the sofa back behind her, deliberately casual. She felt a brief moment of relief. It was best they walk around this elephant.

"You're not priggish," he said. He glanced down the arm that now lay behind her like a live electric fence. "But I suppose you always had that unyielding moral streak." He paused. "That's what broke us, wasn't it?"

He sat up. Tension bristled between them. She looked into the eyes she knew so well. To the outside world Ben Shorter was so confident – arrogant, even; but somehow she'd always been able to hurt him. She regretted that. She didn't know how to bridge the gap but in that moment she wanted to so much.

He leaned in to her.

The moment his lips touched hers was so comforting – delicate, forgiving. A friend's kiss…

His hand slid round her back.

One Christmas her father brought home a glittering carousel – all pink and silver – with a candle in the centre. It was a family ritual; a new decoration for the tree each year. She was three years old and she loved that glittering, revolving carousel, driven by the heat of the candle. She wanted to hold it. Her mother stopped her. That glittering, lovely thing would burn, she said. But she was a child. She picked it up and it burned her and crumpled in her hand. Faith remembered the moment, the loss, the surrender of putting it down.

She felt the pressure of Ben's arm shifting her weight towards him, beneath him.

She was out of control. The half-glass of wine had gone to her head.

She put both hands up against his chest and pushed him away. This was a bad, bad idea!

She leapt to her feet, banging her shins on the coffee table. He just caught his glass of wine before it fell, then righted it, positioning it carefully on the tabletop.

"I should go," he said, standing and picking up his jacket.

He stood with his weight on one foot, body turned towards the door. She didn't know what to say. He looked devastated.

"Well, goodnight." His mouth clamped shut.

She followed him to the door like a chastised puppy. She could still taste him on her mouth. She wanted to stop him, to say something.

She shut the door against the cold night air, paused for several seconds, then walked back through to the other room. He was gone, leaving most of his pizza uneaten, and his wine untouched. She rubbed her head and caught the scratch on her forehead. It hurt. What a truly awful day!

CHAPTER
19

FAITH WOKE ON THE SOFA. What time was it? She drew back
the lounge curtains to let in the morning light and looked at the
clock. Nearly seven o'clock! She couldn't bear the idea of getting
up again after a couple of hours, so she decided to make do with
a bath and coffee.

As she soaked in the bubbles, she dozed. The pieces of the
puzzle shifted about in her head. Was the break-in at Jessica's
connected to Ingram's death?

As Ben had said, nothing but loose ends!

Nothing seemed to connect. She hadn't come across anyone
who didn't like Alistair Ingram. Why should anyone want to
murder such a man?

Because he was too good? That was ridiculous!

The water was cooling. She topped the bath up from the hot
tap, agitating the water to refresh the bubbles.

Pat and her mysterious meetings with Alistair Ingram. She
really wanted to find out about them.

Why not ask her?

That's a bit radical.

But then, do you really believe she is a likely poisoner?

When she thought about it, Faith realized that despite the
churchwarden's sometimes unfortunate manner, there was a part
of her that was warming to Pat. Perhaps she would give her a ring

and see if she would mind her dropping in.

Reinvigorated by her plan, she pulled the plug and reached out for a towel.

The first task of the day was transport, she thought, dressing in her bedroom. She didn't even know the state of her car. As she was thinking about it, her mobile rang. It was Peter.

"The boss's asked me to let you know about your car."

So Ben was keeping his distance after last night. Wasn't that what she'd wanted?

"It's been towed in." Peter gave her the details of the garage and a police incident number for her insurance. Ben might not be talking to her but he had been thorough on her behalf. She asked Peter to convey her thanks; they exchanged a couple of pleasantries and rang off.

She fetched the insurance card from her purse. An hour later she had arranged for a courtesy car to be delivered to her door. She congratulated herself that for once the extra premium on her policy had been worth it.

An oval card table with delicate Georgian legs stood in the window; next to it, a chair was positioned to watch over the green. A bird book and a small pair of binoculars rested on its honey-glazed surface. A large grey cat with dense, fine fur looked up from the sofa.

"That's Mr Marchbanks," said Pat briskly. She indicated an overstuffed Victorian chair opposite with a gracious wave of her plump hand.

"How do you do?" said Faith politely to the cat as she sat down. The seat was hard and slippery. Good for the stomach muscles, she thought, bracing herself. Her eye was caught by three little funeral urns lined up on the mantelpiece. They looked too small to contain a human being. Had Pat divided her husband into three? Pat followed her eye-line.

"Mr Marchbanks' predecessors," she explained. "I suppose it

may seem strange to some but I take comfort in it." She blinked rapidly.

"Of course," Faith said.

Pat shifted in her chair. Faith had a sudden association; it was as if Pat were composing her limbs neatly like her cat.

"I am told you are helping the police with their enquiries," she pronounced.

Faith wasn't sure what to say.

"I also understand," the churchwarden continued in her stately manner, "that there have been comments made about Alistair Ingram's financial past?" The round powdered face was severe.

Who'd told her? And where was Pat going with this? Faith found herself staring into the cup of tea she held. She hadn't tasted it yet. What if Pat *was* a serial poisoner after all? She felt her throat close.

Pat took a deliberate sip from her own cup.

"My husband, Gordon," she stated, "was one of the investors caught in the fraud to which Alistair Ingram's name was linked before he came to Little Worthy. He left me in quite a position." She looked around the room, her expression detached. "I nearly lost this house."

Pat inclined her torso stiffly from the hips. Faith wondered if she wore stays.

"I will tell you the truth, Faith," she confided. "It was a matter of greed. The returns offered were much too good to be true. But then, Gordon always was a fool about money." She sat with her back ramrod straight.

"But I married him and I stood by my bargain to the end," she concluded.

Pat's expression was formidable. Faith considered the departed Gordon and what his life might have been with such a wife.

Pat put her cup down on the saucer dead centre on the coaster on the polished side table.

"That was just about the time Alistair Ingram came here."

"Alistair Ingram was involved in the fraud?" asked Faith.

Pat shook her head vigorously.

"Oh, dear me, no! He was a consultant of some sort."

Pat seemed to approve. She probably thought of a consultant as a superior sort of doctor.

"It all happened while his wife was dying. Alistair told me again and again that he blamed himself for his lack of professional care. *I* never blamed him. He was caring for his wife as a husband should. And after he came here and heard of my troubles he did what he could. He gave me good advice and would never take a penny for it. He steered me towards some sound investments. He encouraged my little talent and I turned things around. Women can be quite good with money too, you know."

Faith looked at Pat's neat-featured face. In the round eyes she caught a glimpse of the effort it cost Mrs Montesque to keep her public mask in place. The woman had dignity. She felt guilty that it had taken her so long to notice it.

"Alistair was a generous man," Pat said gruffly. There were tears in her eyes. "He would come and watch the news with me sometimes. Gordon always liked to watch the six o'clock news. A gin and tonic and the news, it 'settles the appetite'." She gave a little nod, acknowledging her dead husband's phrase. "Alistair would come and watch the news with me and we'd have a little chat about finances. He was very knowledgeable." She gave a tiny, ladylike sniff. Her hands searched around the edges of the cushion of her chair. She came up with a lacy handkerchief and dabbed her button nose. "I shall miss him."

Mr Marchbanks got up and stretched. He walked delicately along the back of the sofa, then jumped into his mistress's lap and positioned herself languidly. His amber eyes fixed Faith with a calm, superior stare. His purr reverberated softly in the room. Pat stroked his fur.

"It's silly getting attached, of course, but they are good companions," she said with a touch of her old briskness. "And one misses them when they're gone."

Faith sat in her courtesy car, thinking about their conversation. Another suspect ruled out. After a week, that's all she seemed to do – convince herself that suspects were not suspect at all. There was something about cars. It kept nagging at the back of her brain. What *is* it?

The car her insurers had provided was small and shiny and smelt of plastic, with a Sat Nav incorporated in the dashboard. She'd never had one of those before. The steering wheel felt tiny between her hands. The garage mechanic had said her own car could be fixed eventually.

Faith gazed idly across the green. The stretch of grass by the car was mossy. I wonder who maintains the green if it's open land, she pondered. Is it like a communal garden or… Moss. The colour and texture reminded her of something. Green bouclé. Sitting in that uncomfortable chair in the bishop's office…

The flying tomato needs a tune-up; it's making a terrible racket…

She heard her own sharp intake of breath. No. That was a crazy idea. Wasn't it?

Like a series of slides, fragments came together. She saw Little Worthy green under that grey sky on the day Trevor died and that dash of red – the old model Ford Escort in dull red parked by the grass. Then the same car standing beyond the TV station vehicle in front of the diocesan offices. And Fred's account of the man crying in his car parked in the dark at the top of Shoesmith's lane. And little Richard Shelley's face as he told them about the sound of the car engine driving away after Jessica's break-in.

She concentrated, recalling the stifling sense of being trapped in that green bouclé chair in the bishop's office. *My wife's old car,* Bishop Anthony had said. *It's always developing some rattle or other.*

How to check? Pat was the one-woman neighbourhood watch. She might know. Faith snatched up her bag and fumbled for her phone. Pat answered on the third ring.

"Pat – it's me again, Faith. I've just thought of something

– you haven't by any chance noticed a strange car around the green recently?" She recalled Fred's account. "Dark blue or maybe red?"

"No. That doesn't ring a bell," Pat said.

The effervescent excitement ebbed. It was a long shot after all.

"Thanks Pat. Sorry to have disturbed you. I just thought I'd ask."

"Not dark blue, but red…" Pat cut across her. "Well, there's that car the bishop's son drives, of course. I've seen him about the village once or twice lately sitting in his old red – Escort or some such, don't they call them? Rather downmarket for a man of his background, but then, some charity workers do like to make a point. And I suppose one should make allowances – it's never easy growing up with a limp. Children can be so cruel. Polio as a child."

The rush of adrenaline made Faith feel dizzy. She hardly knew what she said to Pat. She rang off.

The pieces came together like a kaleidoscope pattern. Jessica's failed romance with the married charity worker. Fred had told her how Jessica had volunteered at a diocesan sponsored project in Tanzania that day in the church hall. Then there was Mrs Beech's concern about the state of her son's marriage – dear Lord! It was right under her nose.

But how could it be true? The bishop's son!

Simon Beech limped, Pat said.

A man with a limp…

Doesn't that sound like a murderer?

Don's glass man; the stranger he gave the key to on that Saturday before Alistair Ingram died, the stranger who rocked when he walked.

Alison had told her of her son's illness when he was young. He'd caught something upcountry. She hadn't said what had made her son so ill that they'd had to fly him home from Africa, had she? Faith frowned, trying to remember the conversation with

Mrs Beech at the hospital the day Alistair Ingram died. She didn't think she had mentioned polio, but that must have been it.

Jessica. She had to talk to Jessica. Faith started the car up and drove off at speed, her heart pumping.

CHAPTER
20

THE STREET WAS QUIET. Everyone seemed to be out on their Saturday errands. Jessica's silver car was gone from her driveway. Faith listened to the doorbell chiming inside. There was no answer. She pressed her face against the front window, peering in. The living room was show-home neat. She went round the side of the house to the back door. Just on the off-chance, she tried the door knob. It wasn't locked.

That was worrying, given the recent break-in and Jessica's declared determination to be more security conscious. Faith stood still, listening, every nerve on edge. Silence. Nothing. Except an odour.

The house smelled of bleach. She checked around her. Just inside the door there was one of those plastic sacks charities pushed through the letter box soliciting for donations. Its top flopped open. It was filled with folded bedding, white with a narrow stripe of soft jade. A tall silver pedal bin stood by the fridge. Its lid was held ajar a few inches. In the gap she glimpsed flower stems. She crossed over and pressed the pedal with her foot. A bunch of irises, the blooms still fresh, had been crammed in. Among the leaves twinkled a silver chain. Faith lifted it out – the fish pendant swung between her fingers. She stared at it for a moment.

A man in his thirties to forties, with short brown to fair hair.

That was Di's description – and it matched Don's glass man.

Her foot was still on the pedal holding the lid open. There was a torn section of postcard poking up between the stems. She fished it out and found another and another. A minute later she had retrieved seven fragments of card. She reassembled them on the countertop, moving them about to form a picture.

It was a view of Lymington, separated into four quarters showing different aspects of the town. She turned the pieces over. The message on the back was stained and smudged but quite clear: *I'm waiting for you by the sea.*

There was no signature or date or address. Just the Christian symbol of a stylized fish. The postmark was barely legible. It had been posted, first class, from Winchester the day before.

The phone was on the wall by the fridge. Next to it was pinned a whitewashed wooden board and on it, a neatly typed list of telephone numbers. One was helpfully labelled "Diana". Faith picked up the receiver and dialled.

"Di – Faith Morgan. Hi! I'm glad I've caught you. I wonder, have you seen Jessica today? Only I've just come to call on her and the back door's open but no sign of her."

"Bad girl! I swear she is so vague some times," Di responded playfully. "She's gone shopping, I think. I saw her drive out – maybe half an hour ago?"

"Thanks."

She broke the connection and got out her mobile. She couldn't remember; did she have it?

Yes. There it was: "Jessica". She waited as the phone rang. On the sixth ring it picked up.

"*The person you've called is unable to come to the phone,*" intoned the irritating electronic lady. Faith waited impatiently for the beep.

"Jessica, it's Faith. Please call me when you have a moment. It's important."

She stood by the phone, thinking. Now where had she seen them? Of course. She made a beeline for the study and found

Jessica's set of telephone directories neatly aligned on a blond wood bookcase.

It was a long shot. Many bishops were ex-directory, especially their retirement homes, but it was worth a try. Bee... Beeby... Beech. There it was. Blossom Cottage, Lymington. She jotted down the address.

Jessica's laptop was on the desk. She flipped it open and turned it on. It looked as though she had wireless connection. The box was up on the bookcase by the window. She waited impatiently for the thing to load. A message flag popped at the bottom of the screen. *Wireless Network Connection Connected.* Good.

She Googled the Royal Mail site and entered the address. Like magic the postcode came up. She noted it down beside the address. She never could trust her memory on such things; she always second-guessed herself.

Back in the kitchen, she made a quick search of drawers and got lucky. A spare set of keys. She was glad to be able to lock the door behind her. Jessica had had too many uninvited visitors of late.

She entered the postcode in the Sat Nav on the dashboard, and started up the engine.

Turn right at... said a woman's disembodied and slightly patronizing voice. This just might work.

The route from Jessica's to Lymington seemed to involve an awful lot of directions; turn here, look out for approaching junction there. It took all of Faith's concentration to follow the instructions enunciated by the implacable digital voice. She had been driving for some time when it occurred to her that she hadn't told anyone where she was going. She should ring Ben. The thought of last night's incident made her shy away from the thought. She would take the coward's way out and ring Peter.

She spotted a lay-by and pulled over. The phone seemed to ring for ever, and then at last he picked up.

"You have reached the message service for Sergeant Peter Gray..."

"Peter, it's Faith. I'm pretty sure it's Simon Beech. I think he may have Jessica at the cottage in Lymington…" Her phone was dead.

She stared at it disbelievingly. What was going on? Then she remembered the battery. The display bar was empty. She'd forgotten to charge it. How could she be such an idiot! She had meant to do it, but what with the car crash and Ben…

It was all Ben's fault. He had to barge in and distract her.

Calm down. She looked about. She was in a country lane. There was no pub or shop in sight. She should find a phone but she was haunted by a sense of urgency. Jessica had more than half an hour's start on her. If she was right, Jessica had gone to face a killer. She had to catch up with her.

She put the car in gear and set off. She'd be bound to pass a phone box or pub soon, she reasoned to herself; she could ring from there. She wasn't absolutely sure when the phone had cut out. She *thought* she'd recorded the key information before the battery died.

She glimpsed the sea twinkling on the horizon. *A cottage by the sea…*

"Turn right at the next junction by the golf course," intoned the Sat Nav. Faith noted the golf course rolling out to her right. She thought of those stories about hapless humans driving into lakes, mesmerized by the authority of their Sat Navs. Was this really going to work?

She almost missed it. There was a rustic oak sign set in a hedge with "Blossom Cottage" burned into it in hot poker work. She slammed on the brakes. A car hooted indignantly behind her, and accelerated past with a furious roar of its engine. She checked the road guiltily. It was clear. She found a safe spot and made a careful U-turn.

Blossom Cottage was a late nineteenth-century brick cottage with a half-moon gravel drive. Roses spilled out from a wild-looking bush beside the narrow porch. *An aphid problem.* Jessica's silver car was parked at an angle in front of the door.

Its boot stood open.

Faith glanced into the boot. The bright beach bag gleamed out of the shadows. It was hardly four days ago that I caught her with that, she thought. So much had happened so fast.

There was something else in the boot. A long, flat green canvas case. Trevor Shoesmith's missing shotgun. Faith leaned in and poked it. It was empty.

She should have known. If Jessica was going to take the pesticide that morning to stop Trevor hurting himself, why wouldn't she take the gun?

She caught a glimpse of movement through the window. She went up to the front door. It was slightly ajar. She thought she heard a voice inside, its tone insistent. She pushed the cool wood cautiously. There was a narrow hall and an open doorway to the left. She saw a shadow move on the wall. She stepped into the doorway.

"Hello. Where did you get that gun?" she heard herself ask conversationally.

CHAPTER

JESSICA WAS STANDING IN THE FAR CORNER of the room away from the window. She was holding a shotgun at waist height. It was pointed at a man sitting in a leather-upholstered club chair; a man with cropped fairish-brown hair, tanned skin and his mother's pale round eyes. Simon Beech.

"It's Trevor's," Jessica answered.

"You took it?" asked Faith.

Jessica glanced at her with a flicker of impatience.

"I thought he might hurt himself with it. I put it in the boot of my car."

"You had it all this time?"

"What's she doing here?" Simon's voice was querulous. Faith looked at him incredulously. He thought she was intruding?

"Faith's my friend."

Well, that's a relief, thought Faith. And a start... What were the odds that the gun was loaded? What was the likelihood Jessica even knew how to load it? Faith didn't recall seeing any cartridges in that boot. She cursed herself for not checking more closely.

"He stalked me!" Jessica seemed to have her right hand in the correct position around the trigger guard. What was the likelihood of her being familiar with shotguns? "He broke into my house!"

The shotgun bobbed alarmingly. Faith made a warning gesture, but Jessica was too incensed to notice. Simon leaned forward in his chair. As he moved, Faith noticed the built-up shoe on his right foot.

"I had to let you know I'd come back for you," he said earnestly. "I love you…"

Jessica took a little step towards him, the barrel of the gun pointed at his face.

"That's not love!" her voice rasped. A different creature had sprung up inside the pretty, meek woman. It stretched the skin across the bones of her face and pointed her chin. "It's perverted," she spat.

She glanced at Faith.

"You know about him?"

"The charity worker who gave you the irises."

Jessica nodded sharply.

"The fake. How long have you known?"

"I've only just put it together. I called at your house. I saw the kitchen."

"He broke in and got into my bed," she said with revulsion.

So that explains the bedding.

"And he left the flowers?" Faith asked. "I wondered about that jug they were in; it didn't look like your choice." She worked hard to keep her tone conversational, but out of the corner of her eye Faith never lost sight of the gun.

Jessica tossed her head and made a scornful sound. They were both standing watching Simon as they talked. He looked perplexed, his eyes shifting from one to the other.

"Who is she?" he asked Jessica.

"I'm Faith Morgan. Your father asked me to come and cover St James's…" She trailed off, thinking of the many ways that sentence might hit a nerve. She glanced at Jessica. She seemed unperturbed.

"She came to me, you know." Simon's manner changed. It was almost as if they were chatting at some weird social occasion. "It was out in Tanzania. She volunteered to help. She's wonderful with finances." His admiration had a sickly quality. There was something about the tone of his delivery that made Faith's skin creep.

"There was a crisis. I was about to lose the project. But she came, like an angel, and saved me."

"I didn't save you…" Jessica hissed.

"But you tried," he shot back.

"The finances were unsustainable." Jessica addressed Faith as if he hadn't spoken. "He was borrowing against expectations. He convinced me God would find a way, but I should have known. Once I'd gone through the books it was obvious – except I didn't want to see it."

Simon's eyes were locked in adoration on Jessica.

"You don't listen to me!" she cried sharply. "You never listened to me. You don't know me. You just talk and talk and talk."

Simon looked vaguely smug. *He's enjoying the attention*, thought Faith. *Doesn't he realize that gun could go off?*

"What are you?' Jessica scoffed. "I thought you were a decent man."

"You know I am." His voice was cajoling. "You couldn't love me otherwise. And you do love me – you know you do. We're each other's salvation."

"Alistair was my salvation, not you! He knew me." Her voice caught and she blinked back tears.

"Alistair Ingram!" Simon exclaimed. His skin flushed under the tan. "The great man! Enough of him!"

He wasn't looking at them any more. He was talking in a world of his own.

"Ingram can help you sort out your finances," he said in a savage parody of someone. "Dear Bishop Daddy! He has no idea. He sends me out there and there's never enough money…" He looked up at Jessica, pleading. "I saw you together. I saw you through the window. What kind of priest is that," he demanded, glaring at Faith briefly, "seducing a vulnerable woman? After all I've done. He seduced you."

After all I've done, thought Faith. She felt cold.

"I nearly despaired that night. I thought, what can I do? Then at dinner they were going on about her roses. Chemicals poison the land, he said; but sometimes nothing else will rid you of the pests, she said. They eat all the beauty away. So I put it in God's hands."

"You poisoned him?" Faith asked quietly.

His eyes flicked up to her face.

"A sip of that wine wouldn't have killed a good man," he said dismissively. "It was God's will. I saw signs." He focused on the middle distance, chanting to himself. "She was pulling me down. Everything was collapsing. 'Let it go,' she said. She didn't understand. He called me home, did you know that? It was in God's hands; I left it in God's hands."

Faith wasn't sure why, but he seemed to feel the need to convince her. She wondered what response would be best calculated to calm him. She was worried about the effect his rising hysteria was having on Jessica. The more he appeared like a crazed monster, the more likely she would be to do something stupid. While at Hendon, Faith had been taught how to disarm a suspect at close range, but that was so long ago. And they'd known the guns weren't loaded. The weapon in Jessica's shaking hands seemed like a creature in its own right – something alive; deadly.

"It was because of her, of course. She betrayed me. She wrote to Mother. So *Daddy*," Simon spat the word out, loaded with fury, "decided I need to be taken in hand!"

Dread caught Faith by the throat.

"Who betrayed you?" she asked softly.

Something flickered in the pale eyes. He clamped his mouth shut. He turned his attention back to Jessica.

"I went to the church. I thought, if I can pray there God will tell me what to do. He would give me a sign. And he did. The door was locked, but that boy gave me the key. He showed me where it was kept. All doors were unlocked for me, you see. And there was the lamb – the lamb cut out of the wall and put on the ground for slaughter. I followed the signs. Simple faith. When I went in the next morning, no one saw me. No one stopped me. God blinded them."

"Shut up!" shouted Jessica.

"Simple faith," Simon repeated solemnly.

Faith glanced at Jessica. Her face was blank, but her eyes never left the babbling man in the leather chair.

"You know how hard I tried," he whined, "but it was always the same. Bishop and Mrs Anthony – they're such saints. The people, Simon; the people. Look at the purity of their faith," he echoed in a savage sing-song.

He stretched, flicking out his right leg in a nervous tic. The built-up shoe caught on the carpet and jarred.

"And that's what I got. Polio," he said, indicating his foot, his eyes fixed on Faith. He tossed his head. "They had their mission; I was just their boy." He leant forward in his seat towards Jessica. "I came home to find you – just to be with you." Faith thought he was pathetic.

"You tricked me." Jessica's words were crystal clear. "You're a wicked man; a false, slithering thing."

Her hands were shaking more. Faith tried to estimate how much pressure the trigger of a gun like that would take to pull. Was it even loaded? Did Jessica know how to fire it? Faith took a step closer. If she could push the barrel out of the way... But what then? What about Simon?

"But I love you..."

Don't say that! The exclamation reverberated so loudly inside her own head that Faith wondered if she had spoken aloud.

"You don't love me!" The gun jumped in Jessica's hands. "Alistair loved me, and you murdered him." She aimed the gun at his head. Faith heard the click as Jessica cocked the hammer. Her chest fell as she expelled her breath. *So she knows how to fire a gun.*

"Jessica." Faith was amazed how calm her voice sounded; she wasn't sure where the calmness came from. "Jessica – isn't this what he wants?"

Jessica frowned. "Alistair?"

"No. Simon. Look at him."

"He's destroyed everything."

"No. Not yet. He hasn't destroyed you – not unless you pull that trigger."

"Don't!" Jessica cut her off. "He's damned me. He's destroyed good men. I'm going to make him pay."

Faith glanced at the man Jessica regarded as evil sitting at the other end of the gun. He was so ordinary – except his eyes were sparkling and his cheeks were flushed. She felt a surge of revulsion. He's getting off on this!

"Jessica – Jessica!" She desperately wanted her to hear. She could almost feel the tide of misery sucking them out into a sea of wretchedness. "Don't let him win. Can't you see that's what he wants?"

Jessica's head turned a fraction towards her, but her eyes were still pinned on Simon Beech. Faith took another step towards her. Another yard and she might be able to reach the gun, as long as she didn't startle her and set it off by accident.

"Look at him. He wants you to go over the cliff with him. Together."

Jessica's expression flickered at the word.

"Yes, together. You kill him and you and he are together. You'll never be rid of him."

The sound of distant sirens encroached on her consciousness. Faith ached with the effort it took to concentrate on Jessica's face while keeping in sight, at the periphery of her vision, the hands holding that gun. She must be getting so tired of holding the gun up like that. Shotguns weren't light.

"But I want to die," Jessica whispered. Her finger was wrapped around the trigger.

Simon smiled. Don't do that! Faith thought crossly. Does he expect to die?

The sirens grew louder.

"Don't you smile at me!" Jessica shouted. "Do you think this isn't loaded? Do you think I won't?"

She cuddled the gun tight against her cheek, and Faith braced herself for the shot. Then Jessica seemed to relax. She lowered the gun to her hip. As Faith exhaled, she saw Jessica's arm tense.

The sound was physical in the containment of the room. Plaster flew up just to the right above Simon's head. A picture fell, its glass shattering across the carpet.

So it is loaded, thought Faith, her ears ringing. One barrel to go.

A car – no, more than one car – pulled up outside. Doors slammed one after the other. Faith took a step back to look through the window.

"The police are outside," she said.

Through the window, she saw Ben and her heart leapt. He was running towards the cottage.

Simon was sitting in the leather chair with a startled expression on his face, his hair and shoulders white with plaster dust.

Jessica's hands dropped the gun. Faith's heart dropped with it. She just managed to catch it before it hit the ground. She took a deep breath and broke it open. The second barrel was loaded.

"We don't want that, do we?" she heard herself say, like some fussy maiden aunt. With an eye on Simon Beech, she put her arm around Jessica. "It's all right," she murmured across the top of her silky blonde head. Jessica's breath was noisy. She could feel it puff, warm against her neck. "You'll be all right."

Ben strode through the door, heedless of his own safety. His hand touched Faith's shoulder and she met his anxious eyes with a small nod. He was followed by a policeman dressed in full flak jacket and protective gear. Faith handed the policeman the open shotgun. She was glad to be rid of its weight. The room filled with uniformed constables. A couple took Jessica away to another room; others helped Simon Beech to his feet. He was shaking but unhurt. The room was too crowded and the smell of cordite was making Faith feel sick. She had to get outside.

Ben followed her out. His jawline was stiff.

"Did you get my message?" she asked him.

"Got a call from Tanzania," he said.

She took a deep breath. "Celia Beech?"

He nodded, grimly. "What message?" he asked belatedly.

"I thought I'd left a message on Peter's phone, about Jessica and coming here, but my battery died."

His expression said everything. She had been an utter fool.

"Right." The word was heavy with the pressure of his self-control. She braced herself. "What the hell were you thinking of?" The energy in his voice had physical force. She almost recoiled. Her defences sprang into place.

"I was fine," she said crossly. "It was Jessica."

"A distraught woman with a loaded shotgun, and a murderer?" he snapped back.

"What? You'd have been any safer than me?"

He frowned and lowered his voice.

"I'm paid for it," he growled.

He reached out to touch her hand, skin to skin.

"So no damage from that shot blast, then?"

"Some plasterwork's distressed.'

He rewarded her joke with a lopsided smile. She cleared her throat. She hoped her voice was steady.

"So they found Celia?"

He nodded.

"In a drainage ditch not far from the marital home."

"So he tried to hide the body."

Simon Beech had been sane enough to try to cover his tracks.

"We're assuming it was him?" queried Ben.

"Yes." She was certain of it. "I think so."

She betrayed me. She wrote to Mother.

Another police car drew up. Bishop Anthony and Alison got out.

"Damn!" said Ben.

"Yeah."

Tragedy had driven the last vestige of colour from Alison Beech. She stood watching the constable as he guided her son into the car. Simon Beech was crying, his hands clenched down by his sides. Faith stood alongside his mother feeling wordless and inadequate.

"I knew something was terribly wrong," Alison murmured. Her eyes looked at nothing Faith could see. "But not this, not this."

Bishop Anthony took her arm. "Now, Mother, we'll find a way. We'll find a way."

Mrs Beech straightened up. She separated herself carefully from her husband. Walking mechanically, she crossed over to the police car where her son sat in the back, while the officer spoke on the radio.

Love's front line, Faith thought. How can God cope with this?

Alison touched her son's shoulder. He reached up and grabbed her hand and hung on to it, sobbing. Faith could see the tremors pass through Alison with each sob.

Tomorrow was Palm Sunday, Faith realized with a lurch. She was taking the service. "I'm not sure my faith's up to this," she said out loud.

Ben's hand cradled her neck. He was pulling her towards him. Somewhere inside she braced herself – but he just dropped a kiss on the top her head and let her go.

"It's OK," he said above her. "No one else heard that."

CHAPTER

By six o'clock that same day, Faith was sitting in Ruth's spare room with the Cabbage Patch dolls looming over her, staring at the blank screen of her laptop. In less than sixteen hours she would be preaching on Palm Sunday. As curate of St Michael's back in Birmingham, her Palm Sunday processions had been a highlight of the season. The cursor blinked at her reproachfully. She'd been sitting here for twenty minutes. She had plenty to say about sin; it was the hopeful celebration she was short on right now.

To be honest, for all her successes in that line, she had a problem with Palm Sunday. She was uncomfortable with the re-enactment of the fair-weather crowds acclaiming Jesus as a celebrity as he entered Jerusalem – the same crowds who would turn on him, a mere five days later, baying for his blood. The message seemed to be "you can't trust humanity; it lets you down".

She'd been able to sit down briefly with Jessica after the hour or so of police interviews.

"When I get through this, I'm going away," she'd said. "I want a new start."

"But you have friends here."

Jessica had glanced at Faith bleakly, and then her face had softened. "Thank you. But I don't want to be known like this.

Maybe I'll come back when all this has died down."

"What will you do?" Faith had asked.

"A friend was talking about a job in an accountancy practice in Cheshire."

"Dealing with footballers' wives and their fortunes?"

Jessica had laughed humourlessly. "I thought I'd try the material life for a while."

Perhaps she was right. Faith had thought of Simon Beech. People can go mad looking for God too hard, she'd thought.

The harsh overhead light had caught Jessica's hair. The carefully tinted blonde highlights were growing out. The naïve bloom she'd had when Faith had first set eyes on her was gone. She'd seemed somehow reduced and refined to an essence of herself. Faith had decided she liked what remained.

Jessica had looked straight at her.

"Do you think I'll survive this?" she'd asked.

"Yes. I know you will."

They'd sat silent together in the blank room. They'd been through so much together of late, it was quite peaceful.

It's not about fixing things; sometimes it's about being alongside in the midst.

The next morning she was there, in the church, half an hour early. She walked through the empty nave in her cassock, listening to the peaceful sounds of Fred and Pat laying out service sheets and hymnals. She came to a halt before the altar. The three windows behind were perfectly proportioned. A harmony of light and stone and glass, and in the middle, the cross.

It's about love.

But what if there is no truth to it?

It's a gamble, said a calming voice.

She looked back. Fred and Pat had their heads together. They were laughing at some joke. They're worth the gamble, she thought.

In the event, the service was rather upbeat. Peter brought his wife, Sandra, and their two little boys. Peter proved himself useful as an animal wrangler when the donkey Sue had borrowed from a sanctuary down the road turned out to be a little skittish. With Peter's coaxing, the donkey became quite the star of the show – along with Clarissa and Timothy's little girl, Alisha, who rode on his back, beaming, as the Christ figure. They all sang and waved palm crosses. And Faith's sermon seemed to go down quite well. It's the people who make the celebration, she thought.

She didn't mention the events at Blossom Cottage. She overheard Fred telling Pat that Jessica had been called away. They would read about it in the papers soon enough; it wasn't her story to tell.

She was saying goodbye at the church door when Ben came up the path.

"Fancy meeting you here."

"Did you want me for something?" she asked.

He paused and then let that one pass.

"No. Peter. We've got a new case."

"He's taking the donkey home. He should be back in a few minutes."

Ben looked down his nose at her.

"Barely a week and I see you've got my sergeant under your thumb."

They strolled a few yards round the now familiar circuit. The chestnut pony no longer stood in the field of weeds. It had gone, along with the rest of Trevor Shoesmith's stock, to an RSPCA sanctuary in Dorset. Faith wondered if Luke McIvor would finally get the land. He'd probably do better by it.

"Will Simon be extradited to Tanzania?" she asked.

"Not sure. Bishop Anthony has some connections. My guess is that the defence will plead insanity. As long as he's locked up, the African authorities may be willing to let the British courts handle it."

He swept a look up and down her clerical surplice and stole.

"So, how was it?" he asked.

"OK," she smiled. "Faith finds a way."

He pulled a face. A poor joke, but her own. The clematis flowers had dropped. Petals lay in a drift at the foot of the grey wall.

"Next up, Holy Week," she said.

"I've been asking around," he said. "Holy Week's supposed to be about death and crucifixion, isn't it? Seems appropriate…"

She stared at him for a moment. He was deliberately looking away from her across the empty field. She bumped him lightly with her shoulder.

"You know, you keep surprising me," she said.

His eyes crinkled at the sides. "Well, that's a start, I suppose."

Peter was waving at them from the church gate.

"Must be off."

He gave her a mock RAF salute. She watched his familiar figure disappear down the path.

"Vicar!"

Faith took a big breath and turned.

"Pat," she said. "How can I help you?"

"The kiddies enjoyed the service, I think." Pat somehow managed to infuse the compliment with an element of disapproval. "I just wanted to let you know that yesterday the glass restorers came to fetch away that panel at last. I had a firm word," she looked coyly at Faith from under her lashes, "if you know what I mean; and they swore to me they'd have it back in a week or two. A week, I told them; a week is what you'll get, or I'll be on to you. I'd like to see it in for Easter. That boarded up window's an eyesore."

So the Lamb of God was on its way to being reinstated at St James's Little Worthy. That was a pleasing idea.

Easter. Faith looked up at the mellow stone sides of St James's planted so neat and personable in its churchyard. The thought of celebrating Easter in her own church filled her with a rush of pride and exhilaration. She was home. She glanced down affectionately at her churchwarden. A member of her congregation, she thought sentimentally; her family.

"I am planning something very special for the altar." Pat was as enthusiastic as Faith had ever seen her. "A big, bold display. It's such a treat to have an excellent preacher like Canon Arbuthnot coming to take our Easter service. It's important to make an effort."

Faith looked down at the perfectly coiffed head bobbing beside her, and smiled.

"That would be lovely," she said.